[The World of a Few Minutes Ago]

MADE IN MICHIGAN WRITERS SERIES

General Editors
Michael Delp, Interlochen Center for the Arts
M. L. Liebler, Wayne State University

Advisory Editors
Melba Joyce Boyd
Wayne State University

Stuart Dybek
Western Michigan University

Kathleen Glynn

Jerry Herron
Wayne State University

Laura Kasischke
University of Michigan

Frank Rashid
Marygrove College

Doug Stanton
Author of *In Harm's Way*

*A complete listing of the books in this series
can be found online at wsupress.wayne.edu*

[The World of a Few Minutes Ago]

Stories by
JACK DRISCOLL

Wayne State University Press
Detroit

© 2012 by Wayne State University Press, Detroit, Michigan
48201. All rights reserved. No part of this book may be re-
produced without formal permission. Manufactured in the
United States of America.

16 15 14 13 12   5 4 3 2 1

Library of Congress Cataloging-in-Publication Data

Driscoll, Jack, 1946–
The world of a few minutes ago : stories / by Jack Driscoll.
p. cm. — (Made in Michigan writers series)
ISBN 978-0-8143-3612-0 (pbk. : alk. paper)
1. Domestic fiction, American. I. Title.
PS3554.R496W67 2012
813'.54—dc22
2011023549

Typeset by Maya Rhodes
Composed in Apollo MT

In memory of my friend EWAN COLLINS

And for LOIS, always,
around whom the constellations align

And did you get what
You wanted from this life, even so?
I did.
And what did you want?
To call myself beloved,
To feel myself beloved on the earth.

RAYMOND CARVER

[Contents]

[Acknowledgments]

These stories, sometimes in a slightly different form, appeared in the following publications:

"This Season of Mercy" in *Alaska Quarterly Review*; "Prowlers," "The Dangerous Lay of the Land," and "Sky Riders" in the *Georgia Review*; "Long After the Sons Go Missing" in *Gray's Sporting Journal*; "Saint Ours" and "After Everyone Else Has Left" in the *Idaho Review*, the latter story also excerpted in *Portland Monthly* magazine; "Travel Advisory," under the title "The Hermit Journals," in *Indiana Review*; "Wonder," and "The World of a Few Minutes Ago" in the *Southern Review*.

"Prowlers" was reprinted in the 2009 *Pushcart Prize Anthology*.

My heartfelt thanks to the editors, and to Shelley Washburn, the Pacific University faculty and staff, my longtime colleagues at the Interlochen Center for the Arts, and to my students, former and current, all of them everywhere.

[Prowlers]

THERE'S A LADDER that leans against the back of the house, a sort of stairway to the roof where Marley-Anne and I sometimes sit after another donnybrook. You know the kind, that whump of words that leaves you dumbstruck and hurt and in the silent nightlong aftermath startled almost dead. Things that should never be spoken to a spouse you're crazy in love with—no matter what.

Yeah, that's us, Mr. and Mrs. Reilly Jack. It's not that the air is thin or pure up here, not in mid-August with all that heat locked in the shingles. It's just that we can't be inside after we've clarified in no uncertain terms the often fragile arrangement of our marriage. And right there's the irony, given that we fill up on each other morning, noon, and night—excepting during these glitches, of course, when we reassert our separateness, and all the more since we've started breaking into houses.

B&E artists, as Marley-Anne calls us, and that's fine with me, though never before in our history had we made off with somebody's horse. Tonight, though, a large mammal is grazing ten feet below us in our small, fenced-in backyard. This kind of incident quick-voids a lease, and we signed ours ten months ago with a sweet-deal option to buy. A simple three-bedroom starter ranch with a carport, situated on an irregular quarter acre where in the light of day we present ourselves as your ordinary small-town underachievers. And that pretty much identifies the demographic hereabouts: white, blue-collar, Pet Planet employed. I'd feed their C-grade canned to my rescue mutt any day of the week if I could only sweet-talk Marley-Anne into someday getting one.

I drive a forklift, which may or may not be a lifelong job but, if so, I'm fine with that future, my ambitions being somewhat less than insistent. Marley-Anne, on the other hand, is a woman of magnum potential, tall and funny and smart as the dickens, and I buy her things so as not to leave her wanting. Last week, a blue moonstone commemorating our ten-year anniversary, paid for up front in full by yours truly.

Anything her maverick heart desires, and I'll gladly work as much swing-shift or graveyard overtime as need be, though what excites Marley-Anne . . . well, let me put it this way: there's a river nearby and a bunch of fancy waterfront homes back in there, and those are the ones we stake out and prowl.

The first time was not by design. The declining late winter afternoon was almost gone, and Marley-Anne riding shotgun said, "Stop." She said, "Back up," and when I did she pointed at a Real Estate One sign advertising an open house, all angles and stone chimneys and windows that reflected the gray sky. "That's tomorrow," I said. "Sunday." And without another word she was outside, breaking trail up the unshoveled walkway, the snow lighter but still falling, and her ponytail swaying from side to side.

She's like that, impulsive and unpredictable, and I swear I looked away—a couple of seconds max—and next thing I know she's holding a key between her index finger and thumb, and waving for me to come on, hurry up, Reilly Jack. Hurry up, like she'd been authorized to provide me a private showing of this mansion listed at a million-two or million-three—easy—and for sure not targeting the likes of us. I left the pickup running, heater on full blast, and when I reached Marley-Anne I said, "Where'd you find that?" Meaning the key, and she pointed to the fancy brass lock, and I said, "Whoever forgot it there is coming back. Count on it."

"We'll be long gone by then. A spot inspection and besides I have to pee," she said, her knees squeezed together. "You might as well come in out of the cold, don't you think?"

"Here's fine," I said. "This is as far as I go, Marley-Anne. No kidding, so how about you just pee and flush and let's get the fuck off Dream Street, okay?"

What's clear to me is that my mind's always at its worst in the waiting. Always, no matter what, and a full elapsing ten minutes is a long while to imagine your wife alone in somebody else's domicile. I didn't knock or ring the doorbell. I stepped inside and walked through the maze of more empty living space than I had ever seen or imagined. Rooms entirely absent of furniture and mirrors, and the walls and ceilings so white I squinted, the edges of my vision blurring like I was searching for someone lost in a storm or squall.

"Marley-Anne," I said, her name echoing down hallways and up staircases and around the crazy asymmetries of custom-built corners jutting out everywhere like a labyrinth. Then more firmly asserted until I was shouting, hands cupped around my mouth, "Marley-Anne, Marley-Anne, answer me. Please. It's me, Reilly Jack."

I found her in the farthest far reaches of the second floor, staring out a window at the sweep of snow across the river. She was shivering, and I picked up her jacket and scarf off the floor. "What are you doing?" I asked, and all she said back was, "Wow. Is that something or what?" and I thought, Oh fuck. I thought, Here we go, sweet Jesus, wondering how long this time before she'd plummet again.

We're more careful now, and whenever we suit up it's all in black, though on nights like this with the sky so bright, we should always detour to the dump with a six-pack of cold ones and watch for the bears that never arrive. Maybe listen to Mickey Gilley or Johnny Cash and make out like when we first started dating back in high school, me a senior and Marley-Anne a junior, and each minute spent together defining everything I ever wanted in my life. Against the long-term odds we stuck. We're twenty-nine and twenty-eight, respectively, proving that young love isn't all about dick and daydreams and growing up unrenowned and lonesome. Just last month, in the adrenaline rush of being alone in some strangers' lavish master bedroom, we found ourselves going at it in full layout on their vibrating king-size. Satin sheets the color of new aluminum and a mirror on the ceiling, and I swear to God we left panting and breathless. You talk about making a score . . . that was it, our greatest sex ever. In and out like pros, and the empty bed still gyrating like a seizure.

Mostly we don't loot anything. We do it—ask Marley-Anne—for the sudden rush and flutter. Sure, the occasional bottle of sweet port to celebrate, and once—just the one time—I cribbed a padded-shoulder, double-breasted seersucker suit exactly my size. But I ended up wearing instead the deep shame of my action, so the second time we broke in there I hung the suit back up where I'd originally swiped it, like it was freshly back from the dry cleaners and hanging again in that huge walk-in closet. We're talking smack-dab on the same naked white plastic hanger.

Now and again Marley-Anne will cop a hardcover book if the title sounds intriguing. *The Lives of the Saints*, that's one that I remember held her full attention from beginning to end. Unlike me she's an avid reader; her degree of retention you would not believe. She literally burns through books, speed-reading sometimes two per night, so why *not* cut down on the cost? As she points out, these are filthy-rich people completely unaware of our immanence, and what's it to them anyway, these gobble-jobs with all their New World bucks?

I'd rather not, I sometimes tell her, that's all. It just feels wrong.

Then I throw in the towel because the bottom line is whatever makes her happy. But grand theft? Jesus H., that sure never crossed my mind, not once in all the break-ins. (I'd say twenty by now, in case anyone's counting.) I'm the lightweight half in the mix, more an accessory along for the ride, though of my own free will I grant you, and without heavy pressure anymore, and so no less guilty. No gloves, either, and if anyone has ever dusted for fingerprints they've no doubt found ours everywhere.

Foolhardy, I know, and in a show of hands at this late juncture I'd still vote for probing our imaginations in more conventional, stay-at-home married ways. Like curling up together on the couch for Tigers baseball or possibly resuming that conversation about someday having kids. She would say two would be satisfactory. I'd say that'd be great. I'd be riding high on numbers like that. But all I have to do is observe how Marley-Anne licks the salt rim of a margarita glass, and I comprehend all over again her arrested maternal development and why I've continued against my better judgment to follow her anywhere, body and soul, pregnant or not.

That doesn't mean I don't get pissed, but I do so infrequently and always in proportion to the moment or event that just might get us nailed or possibly even gutshot. And how could I—a husband whose idealized version of the perfect wife is the woman he married and adores—ever live with that? I figure a successful crime life is all about minimizing the risks so nobody puts a price on your head or even looks at you crosswise. That's it in simple English, though try explaining "simple" to a mind with transmitters and beta waves like Marley-Anne's.

Not that she planned on heisting someone's goddamn paint, because forward-thinking she'll never be, and accusations to that effect only serve to aggravate an already tenuous situation. All I'm saying is that a bridle was hanging on the paddock post, and next thing I knew she was cantering bareback out the fucking gate and down the driveway like Hiawatha minus the headband and beaded moccasins. Those are the facts. *Clop-clop-clack* on the blacktop, and in no way is the heightened romance inherent in that image lost on me.

But within seconds she was no more than a vague outline and then altogether out of sight, and me just standing there, shifting from foot to foot, and the constellations strangely spaced and tilted in the dark immensity of so much sky. Good Christ, I thought. Get back here, Marley-Anne, before you get all turned around, which maybe she already had. Or maybe she got thrown or had simply panicked and ditched the horse and stuck to our standing strategy to always rendezvous at the pickup if anything ever fouled.

But she wasn't at the truck when I got back to it. I slow-drove the roads and two-tracks between the fields where the arms of oil wells pumped and wheezed, and where I stopped and climbed into the truck bed and called and called out to her. Nothing. No sign of her at all, at least not until after I'd been home for almost two hours, half-crazed and within minutes of calling 911.

And suddenly there she was, her hair blue-black and shiny as a raven's under that evanescent early morning halo of the street lamp as she rode up to 127 Athens, the gold-plated numerals canted vertically just right of the mail slot. Two hours I'd been waiting, dead nuts out of my gourd with worry. I mean I could hardly even breathe, and all she says is "Whoa," and smiles over at me like, Hey, where's the Instamatic, Reilly Jack? The house was pitch dark behind me, but not the sky afloat with millions of shimmering stars. I could see the sweating brown-and-white rump of the pinto go flat slick as Marley-Anne slid straight off backward and then tied the reins to the porch railing as if it were a hitching post. The mount just stood there swishing its long noisy tail back and forth, its neck outstretched on its oversized head and its oval eyes staring at me full on. And that thick corkscrew tangle of white mane, as if it had been in braids, and nostrils flared big and pink like two identical side-by-side conch shells.

I'd downed a couple of beers and didn't get up from the swing when she came and straddled my lap. Facing me she smelled like welcome to Dodge City in time warp. Oats and hay and horse sweat, a real turnoff and, as usual, zero awareness of what she'd done. Nonetheless, I lifted Marley-Anne's loose hair off her face so I could kiss her cheek in the waning moonlight, that gesture first and foremost to herald her safe arrival home no matter what else I was feeling, which was complex and considerable. Her black jeans on my thighs were not merely damp but soaking wet, and the slow burn I felt up and down my spinal cord was electric.

But that's a moot point if there's a horse matter to broker, and there was, of course: Marley-Anne's fantasy of actually keeping it. Don't ask me where, because that's not how she thinks—never in a real-world context, never ever in black and white. She's all neurons and impulse. Factor in our ritual fast-snap and zipper disrobing of each other during or shortly after a successful caper, and you begin to understand my quandary. She does not cope well with incongruity, most particularly when I'm holding her wrists like I do sometimes, forcing her to concentrate and listen to me up close face-to-face as I attempt to argue reason.

Which is why I'd retreated to the roof, and when she followed maybe a half hour later, a glass of lemonade in hand, I said, "Please, just listen okay? Don't flip out, just concentrate on what I'm saying and talk to me for a minute." Then I paused and said, "I'm dead serious, this is bad, Marley-Anne, you have no comprehension *how* bad but maybe it's solvable if we keep our heads." As in, knock-knock, is anybody fucking home?

She'd heard it all before, a version at least, and fired back just above a whisper, "I can take care of myself, thank you very much."

"No," I said, "you can't, and that's the point. You don't get it. We're in big trouble this time. Serious deep shit and our only ticket out—are you even listening to me?—is to get this horse back to the fucking Ponderosa, and you just might want to stop and think about that."

She said nothing, and the raised vein on my left temple started throbbing as Paint thudded his first engorged turd onto the lawn, which I'd only yesterday mowed and fertilized, and then on hands and knees spread dark red lava stones under the azaleas and around the bougainvillea. All the while, Marley-Anne had stood hypnotized at the kitchen window, re-constelling what she sometimes refers to as this down-in-the-heels place where the two of us exist together on a next-to-nothing collateral line.

It's not the Pierce-Arrow of homes, I agree. Hollow-core doors and a bath and a half, but we're not yet even thirty, and for better or worse most days seem substantial enough and a vast improvement over my growing up in a six-kid household without our dad, who gambled and drank and abandoned us when I was five. I was the youngest, the son named after him, and trust me when I say that Marley-Anne's story—like mine—is pages and pages removed from a fully stocked in-home library and a polished black baby grand, and to tell it otherwise is pure unadulterated fiction. "Maybe in the next lifetime," I said once, and she reminded me how just two weeks prior we'd made love on top of a Steinway in a mansion off Riverview, murder on the knees and shoulder blades but the performance virtuoso. And Marley-Anne seventh-heaven euphoric in hyper-flight back to where we'd hidden the pickup behind a dense red thicket of sumac.

Nothing in measured doses for Marley-Anne, whose penchant for drama is nearly cosmic. Because she's restless her mind goes zooming, then dead-ends double whammy with her job and the sameness of the days. Done in by week's end—that's why we do what we do, operating on the basis that there is no wresting from her the impulsive whirl of human desire and the possibility to dazzle time. Take that away, she's already in thermonuclear meltdown—and believe me, the aftereffects aren't pretty.

She works for Addiction Treatment Services as a nine-to-five receptionist filing forms and changing the stylus on the polygraph. Lazy-ass drunks and dopers, jerk-jobs, and diehard scammers—you know the kind—looking to lighten their sentences, and compared to them Marley-Anne in my book can do no wrong. Her code is to outlive the day terrors hell-bent on killing her with boredom, and because I've so far come up with no other way to rescue her spirit I stand guard while she jimmies back doors and ground-level windows. Or sometimes I'll boost her barefoot from my shoulders onto a second-floor deck where the sliders are rarely locked. In a minute or two she comes downstairs and deactivates the state-of-the-art security system, inviting me in through the front door as though she lives there and residing in such splendor is her right God-given.

"Good evening," she'll say. "Welcome. What desserts do you suppose await us on this night, Reilly Jack?"—as if each unimagined delight has a cherry on top and is all ours for the eating. Then she'll motion me across the threshold and into the dark foyer where we'll stand locking elbows or holding hands like kids until our eyes adjust.

At first I felt grubby and little else, and that next hit was always the place where I didn't want to fall victim to her latest, greatest, heat-seeking version of our happiness. I didn't get it, and I told her so in mid-May after we'd tripped an alarm and the manicured estate grounds lit up like a ballpark or prison yard. I'd never taken flight through such lush bottomland underbrush before, crawling for long stretches, me breathing hard but Marley-Anne merely breath*taken* by the kick of it all, and the two of us muddy and salty with perspiration there in the river mist. No fear or doubts or any remorse, no second thoughts on her part for what we'd gotten ourselves into. It's like we were out waltzing Matilda on the riverbank, and screw you, there's this legal trespass law called riparian rights, and we're well within ours—the attitude that nothing can touch brazen enough, and without another word she was bolt upright and laughing in full retreat. And what I saw there in front of me in each graceful stride was the likelihood of our marriage coming apart right before my eyes.

"That's it," I said to her on the drive home. "No more. Getting fixed like this and unable to stop, we're no better than those addicts, no different at all, and I don't care if it *is* why Eve ate the goddamn apple, Marley-Anne"—an explanation she'd foisted on me one time, to which I'd simply replied, "Baloney to that. I don't care. We'll launch some bottle rockets out the rear window of the pickup if that's what it takes." I meant it, too, as if I could bring the Dead Sea of the sky alive with particles of fiery light that would also get us busted, but at worst on a charge of reckless endangerment, which in these parts we'd survive just fine and possibly be immortalized by in story at the local bars.

"We're going to end up twelve-stepping our way out of rehab," I said. "Plus fines and court costs. It's just a matter of time until somebody closes the distance." All she said back was, "Lower case, Reilly Jack. Entirely lower case."

She's tried everything over the years, from Valium to yoga, but gave up each thing for the relish of what it robbed from her. Not to her face, but in caps to my own way of thinking, I'd call our prowling CRAZY.

So far we'd been blessed with dumb luck the likes of which I wouldn't have believed and couldn't have imagined if I hadn't been kneeling next to Marley-Anne in the green aquatic light of a certain living room, our noses a literal inch away from a recessed wall tank of angelfish. Great big ones, or maybe it was just the way they were magnified, some of them yellow-striped around the gills, and the two of us mesmerized by the hum of the filter as if *we* were suspended underwater and none the wiser to the woman watching us—for how long I haven't the foggiest. But in my mind I sometimes hear that first note eerie and helium-high, though I could barely make out, beyond the banister, who was descending that curved staircase. Not until she'd come ghostlike all the way down and floated toward us, a pistol pointed into her mouth.

Jesus, I thought, shuddering, oh merciful Christ no, but when she squeezed the trigger and wheezed deeply it was only an inhaler, her other hand holding a bathrobe closed at the throat.

"Sylvia?" she said. "Is that you?" And Marley-Anne, without pause or panic, stood up slowly and assented to being whoever this white-haired woman wanted her to be. "Yes," she said, "uh-huh, it's me," as if she'd just flown in from Bangor or Moscow or somewhere else so distant it might take a few days to get readjusted. "I didn't mean to wake you," Marley-Anne said, soft-sounding and genuinely apologetic. "I'm sorry." As cool and calm as cobalt while I'm squeezing handful by handful the humid air until my palms dripped rivulets onto the shiny, lacquered hardwood floor. The woman had to be ninety, no kidding, and had she wept in fear of us or even appeared startled I swear to God the lasting effects would have voided forever my enabling anymore the convolution of such madness.

"There's leftover eggplant parmesan in the fridge—you can heat that up," the woman said, "and beets. Oh, yes, there's beets there too," as if suddenly placing something that had gotten lost somewhere, not unlike Marley-Anne and me, whoever I was standing now beside her all part and parcel of the collective amnesia.

"And you are . . . who again?" the woman asked, and wheezed a second time, and when I shrugged as if I hadn't under these circumstances the slightest clue, she slowly nodded. "I understand," she said. "Really, I do." And she took another step closer and peered at me even harder, as if the proper angle of concentration might supply some vague recollection of this mute and disoriented young man attired in burglar black and suddenly present before her.

"Heaven-sent then?" she said, as if perhaps I was some angel, and then she pointed up at a skylight I hadn't noticed. No moon in sight, but the stars—I swear—aglitter like the flecks of mica I used to find and hold up to the sun when I was a kid, maybe six or seven. I remembered then how my mom sometimes cried my dad's name at night outside by the road for all her children's sakes, and for how certain people we love go missing, and how their eventual return is anything but certain. I remembered lying awake on the top bunk, waiting and waiting for that unmistakable sound of the spring hinge snapping and the screen door slapping shut. I never really knew whether to stay put or go to her. And I remembered this, too: how on the full moon, like clockwork, the midnight light through the window transformed that tiny bedroom into a diorama.

"Emphysema," the woman said. "And to think I never smoked. Not one day in my entire life."

"No, that's true," Marley-Anne said, "you never did. And look at you, all the more radiant because of it."

"But not getting any younger," the woman said, and wheezed again, her voice flutelike this time, her eyes suddenly adrift and staring at nothing. "And Lou, how can that be so soon? Gone ten years,

isn't it ten years tomorrow? Oh, it seems like yesterday, just yesterday
. . ." But she couldn't quite recollect even that far, and Marley-Anne
smiled and palm-cupped the woman's left elbow and escorted her back
upstairs to bed. Recalling the run-down two-story of my boyhood, I
noticed how not a single stair in this house moaned or creaked underfoot.

Standing all alone in the present tense with that school of blank-
eyed fish staring out at me, I whispered, "Un-fucking-believable."
That's all I could think. As absurd as it sounds, these were the inter-
ludes and images Marley-Anne coveted, and in the stolen beauty of
certain moments I had to admit that I did, too.

That's what frightens me now more than anything, even more than
somebody's giant, high-ticket pinto in our illegal possession. But first
things first, and because Marley-Anne's one quarter Cheyenne she's
naturally gifted, or so she claimed when I asked her where she learned
to bridle a horse and ride bareback like that. In profile silhouette, hugging her knees here next to me on the roof, she shows off the slight rise
in her nose and those high chiseled cheekbones. She's long-limbed and
lean and goes one-fifteen fully clothed, and I've already calculated that
the two of us together underweigh John Wayne, who somehow always
managed to boot-find the stirrup and haul his wide, white, and baggy
Hollywood cowboy ass into the saddle. Every single film I felt bad for
the horse, the "He-yuh," and spurs to the ribs, and my intolerance was
inflamed with each galloping frame.

Perhaps another quarter hour of silence has passed when Marley-
Anne takes my hand. Already the faintest predawn trace of the darkness lifting leaves us no choice other than to mount up and vacate the
premises before our neighbors, the Bromwiches, wake and catch us
red-handed. They're friendly and easy enough to like but are also the
type who'd sit heavy on the bell rope for something like this. I can
almost make out the outline of their refurbished 1975 midnight-blue
Chevy Malibu parked in the driveway, a green glow-in-the-dark Saint
Christopher poised on the dash and the whitewalls shining like haloes.

Not wanting to spew any epithet too terrible to retract, neither of us utters a word as we climb down in tandem, the horse whinnying for the very first time when my feet touch the ground. "Easy," I say, right out of some *High Noon*–type western. "Easy, Paint." But Marley-Anne's the one who nuzzles up and palm strokes its spotted throat and sweet-talks its nervousness away. I've ridden a merry-go-round, but that's about it, and I wouldn't mind a chrome pole or a pommel to hold onto. But Marley-Anne's in front on the reins, and with my arms snug around her waist I feel safe and strangely relaxed, Paint's back and flanks as soft as crushed velour. Except for our dangling legs and how high up we are, it's not unlike sitting on a love seat in some stranger's country estate. Marley-Anne heels us into a trot around the far side of the house and across the cracked concrete sidewalk slabs into the empty street. Paint's shod hooves don't spark, but they do reverberate even louder, the morning having cooled, and there's no traffic, this being Sunday and the whole town still asleep.

Marley-Anne's black jeans are not a fashion statement. They're slatted mid-thigh for ventilation, and I consider sliding my hands in there where her muscles are taut, and just the thought ignites my vapors on a grand scale, everything alive and buzzing—including the static crackle in the power lines we've just crossed under, and that must be Casey Banhammer's hound dream-jolted awake and suddenly howling at who knows what, maybe its own flea-bitten hind end, from two blocks over on Cathedral.

We're slow cantering in the opposite direction, toward the eastern horizon of those postcard-perfect houses and away from the land of the Pignatallis and Burchers and Bellavitas, whose double-wides we've never been inside without an invitation to stop by for a couple of Busch Lights and an evening of small talk and cards and pizza. Guys I work with, all plenty decent enough and not a whole lot of tiny print—meaning little or nothing to hide. Marley-Anne negotiates their backyards this way and that. A zigzag through the two or three feet of semi-darkness ahead of us, and the perfect placement of Paint's hoof-pounds thudding down. A weightless transport past gas grills and lawn furniture, and someone's tipped-over silver Schwinn hurtled with ease, the forward lift and thrust squeezing Marley-Anne and me even tighter together.

There are no sentry lights or fancy stone terraces or in-ground swimming pools, though the sheets on the Showalters' clothesline seem an iridescent white glow, and when Marley-Anne says, "Duck," I can feel the breezy cotton blow across my back, that sweet smell of starch and hollyhocks, the only flower my mom could ever grow. Shiny black and blue ones the color of Marley-Anne's windswept hair, and I can smell *it* too when I press my nose against the back of her head.

There's a common-ground lot, a small park with a diamond and backstop, and we're cantering Pony Express across the outfield grass. The field has no bleachers, though sometimes when I walk here at night I imagine my dad sitting alone in the top row. I'm at the plate, a kid again, a late rally on and my head full of banter and cheers and the tight red seams of the baseball rotating slow-motion toward me, waist-high right into my wheelhouse. It could, it just might be, my life re-imagined with a single swing, the ball launched skyward, a streaking comet complete with a pure white rooster tail.

But if you've been deserted the way my dad deserted us, no such fantasies much matter after a while. And what could he say or brag about anyway? Truth told, I don't even remember his voice. It's my mom's crying I hear whenever I think of them together and apart. He might be dead for all I know, which isn't much except that he sure stayed gone both then and now. Marley-Anne and I have never mentioned separation or divorce, an outcome that would surely break me for good. And the notion of her up and leaving unannounced some night is simply way too much for someone of my constitution to even postulate.

We slow to something between a trot and a walk, and Paint isn't frothing or even breathing hard, his ears up and forward like he wants more, wants to go and go and go, and maybe leap some gorge or ravine or canyon or, like Pegasus, sprout wings and soar above this unremarkable northern town. On Cabot Street, under those huge-domed and barely visible sycamores, Marley-Anne has to rein him in, and now he's all chest and high-stepping like a circus horse, his nostrils flared for dragon fire. He's so gorgeous that for a fleeting second I want someone to see us, a small audience we'd dazzle blind with an updated Wild Bill story for them to tell their kids.

We look left toward the Phillips 66 and right toward the all-night Laundromat where nobody's about. We keep to those darker stretches between the streetlights and, where Cass intersects with Columbus, there's the Dairy Queen with its neon sign a blurred crimson. The coast is clear, and we stop in the empty parking lot as if it were a relay station on the old overland route to Sioux Falls or San Francisco.

"So far so good," I say, and when Marley-Anne tips her head back I kiss her wine-smooth lips until she moans.

"Hey," she says, her mouth held open as if a tiny bird might fly out. "Hey," like a throaty chorus in a song. When I smile at her she half smiles back as if to say, We're managing in our way just fine, aren't we, Reilly Jack? You and me, we're going to be okay, aren't we? Isn't that how it all plays out in this latest, unrevised chapter of our lives?

I nod in case this *is* her question, and Paint pirouettes a perfect one-eighty so he's facing out toward East Main. Already one walleyed headlight wavers in the huge double plate-glass window of the Dairy Queen as that first car of the morning passes unaware of us. Otherwise the street is deserted, the yellow blinker by the Holiday Inn not quite done repeating itself. Above, up on I-75, a north-south route to no-where, is that intermittent whine and roar of transport trailers zipping past. But there's an underpass being constructed not far from here, no traffic on it at all, and beyond that the sandpit and some woods with a switchback two-track that will bring us out to County Road 667.

Saint Jerome's Cemetery is no more than another half mile dis-tant from there, and I can almost smell the wild honeysuckle by the caretaker's shack, its galvanized roof painted green, and a spigot and hose and pail to give the horse a drink. The deceased are enclosed by a black wrought-iron fence, and there's a gate where we'll hang the bridle and turn Paint loose to graze between the crosses and headstones, and perhaps some flower wreathes mounding a freshly covered grave. Another somebody dead out of turn, as my mom used to say, no matter their age or circumstance, whenever she read the obituaries. Out of turn, out of sorts, just out and out senseless the way this world imposes no limits on our ruin—she'd say that too. She'd say how it grieved her that nothing lasts. "Nothing, Reilly Jack, if you love it, will ever, ever last." Then she'd turn away from me and on her way out glance back to where I was sitting alone in the airless kitchen.

And what are the chances that I'd end up here instead of in another life sleeping off the aftereffects of a late Saturday night at the Iron Stallion, where all the usual suspects were present and accounted for, and the jukebox so stuffed full of quarters that its jaws were about to unhinge and reimburse every drunken, lonely last one of us still humming along. But *here,* at 5:45 a.m. eastern standard, I kiss Marley-Anne again and our hearts clench and flutter, Marley-Anne shivering and her eyes wide open to meet my gaze. Paint is chomping at the bit to go, and so Marley-Anne gives him his lead, his left front hoof on the sewer cover echoing down East Main like a bell.

Already somebody is peppering his scrambled eggs, somebody sipping her coffee, and what's left of this night is trailing away like a former life. The house we lived in is still there exactly the way we left it, the front door unlocked and the pickup's keys in the ignition. *That* life, before those cloud-swirl white splotches on a certain pinto's neck first quivered under Marley-Anne's touch.

[Wonder]

THEIR NAMES: MITCHELL AND MICHELLE, and I couldn't help but wonder from what little he divulged if all similarities between them ended
there.

She had been his colleague, young and bright and hired right out of
grad school to teach French, but had bailed on academe for an Ameri-
can-speaking career in women's retail. The age gap between them, he
joked, was a mere twelve years. He hadn't, as he put it, *quite* looted
the cradle, and then he described her to me over the phone by quot-
ing Melville's remark on the "rare virtue of interior spaciousness." I'd
fallen pretty far away from phrases like that, but after being recently
paroled, I thought virtue and spaciousness in a woman sounded like a
plus.

I'd been married once myself, briefly, but since then those few
women I believed I could have loved long-term always exited in a
hurry, agreeing to meet me again only in dreams. That included Helen,
my then-wife, who filed on the grounds that she wasn't ready for the

early dark, the direction in which I'd been headed for a major portion of my life, and, even against other more promising worldly designs, possibly still was.

But the bar with the pay phone in back served cheap house drinks at midday, and Grand Forks happened along the way that railroad towns did in my drifting and hiring on as a cutter and welder with every railroad from Union Pacific to Norfolk Southern. So I'd seen these States United and Grand Forks was a far cry from the most god-forsaken place I'd ever been. But it was also where I finally ran out of options and ideas and laid out on the bar my last four twenties, and then tried to visualize if that was enough green for a one-way Greyhound bus ticket back home after almost two decades away.

Mitchell and I go all the way back to grade school, best buddies, and straight sober I might not have asked after all this time if I could put down at his place for a while. Just until I landed a job is what I said, though railroad country Petoskey was not, and I had at present no particular other line of work in mind. I'd gotten hold of Mitchell at his office through the college switchboard, and knowing something about how marriages misfire I figured he'd defer his answer at least until he checked things out with Michelle. Who I'd never met, but the lead lines he threw me were high temperature, and outside the snow kept coming down, and all signs pointed toward northern Michigan.

"Alden," he said, "the spare bedroom is yours. For as long as you need it. You know that. No questions asked." Then he gave me his street address, a neighborhood I used to know, given that I'd grown up just a few blocks away in a household I'd done my best to forget. He said the backdoor key was hidden under a rock in the birdbath, in case I arrived while they were out or away. I told him, "I owe you one," and he said back, "Hey, who's counting, right?"

For sure I had been, an unending tabulation of regrets, as I'd stare sleepless into the void above my cell bunk, swearing to God and to myself a brand new life forthcoming once I was on the outside again. Ninety days, and the prospect of a positive outcome in spite of all those bad choices was my single, solitary focus and comfort. As a fellow jailbird said to me, "You make bottom, there's nowhere but up."

That part of my life Mitchell did not need to hear about, and I hoped never would. I'd sent him hokey, single-sentence, bumtown kinds of postcards just to let him know that I was alive. "And thriving," I'd write. "Thriving and still tossing them back." No return address—not ever—though I suppose the postmarks provided a scattered geographical jigsaw for him to piece together. Now and again a late-night, catch-up phone call, which over time became less frequent, and then nonexistent. So there was a lot of silence to break when I decided finally to dial him up, and more guardedness on both our ends than I'd anticipated. But when I told him where I was calling from he said, "North Dakota?" and laughed a laugh I still recognized. And hearing it again like that, I smiled right through the lingering weariness that the booze hadn't even begun to touch.

Then he mentioned a beginning-level ethics class waiting on him in the next room. Which sounded right—a grown-up version of that dreamy, oddball kid with the brushy hair who always took principled positions on complex moral matters that back then just felt stupid inside my head. Like Nixon's lies. Like Chile and Pinochet, Vietnam and Cambodia, though the only war I cared about was the one that raged and raged inside our house after my dad died unexpectedly when I was thirteen, and my mother remarried badly and way too fast, for which I'd never entirely forgiven her.

Whenever she took sides, it was always with him, a follow-orders kind of tyrant who had no job and no children of his own and boasted nonstop about his seventeen-inch neck and lethal forearms. And who, the day I refused to call him "sir," threatened in his new wife's absence to fill my mouth with the sharp, hooked, snipped-off ends of fence wire. He was forever stretching it around something—around his garden, the carport and doghouse, all around the property, so that the place resembled a compound by the time they sold it and moved away at the tail end of my senior year. Grown and gone, he said, meaning them, not me, and no discussion whatsoever about whether I planned to accompany them to New Hampshire, where he was from. None, and my dad, whom I loved and trusted and missed terribly, buried for what already seemed an eternity in Holy Cross Cemetery. And somewhere in the after-silence of all their sudden departures, I landed a job at Olson's Auto Body, torching off mangled trunks and doors and fenders, the beautiful blue whistle of acetylene fire alive all day deep in my ears.

"Like pure music," I kept insisting to Mitchell one summer when he was home from Ann Arbor. He was about to head back to finish up his degree taking, and after maybe his fourth Rolling Rock he cocked his head in a kind of tin-ear grimace, as if the needle had just skipped sideways across whatever record album we'd been listening to. It was mid-July, blistering hot, and bare-chested he put on my welder's mask and slowly scanned the tiny, third-floor dive—my "high-ground," as he sarcastically called it—that I'd been renting by the week. In a certain odd angle of the lamplight, his pupils through the dark safety glass glowed red behind the reflection of my own pale and distorted face staring back.

"Oh, yeah, like pure music?" he said, and whistled into the throat of an empty beer bottle, his other hand torching the premises—floor and walls and ceiling—the whole ugly place consumed in a magnificent imaginary whoosh of flames. Then he slid the mask up and said, "Let's get you the Christ out of here, Alden," as if he'd torched the premises just so he could save my life.

The air was so thick and heavy it hurt to breathe, but a twelve-pack of ice cold ones—what we called green grenades—hit the spot, and Mitchell insisted, "Sure you do. Just sign up for a couple of evening classes to start, and see how that goes." He said the cerebral world awaited conscientious minds like mine—"definitely"—and that I should take it slow to start. "Ease into it," he said. "Then decide if you're born to that kind of life or not."

But game time for me meant all or nothing, and at twenty-two I figured to make up some distance by brain-busting my way through a full load and, as Mitchell predicted, to some pretty respectable grades. Except in Composition 101, where every interminable misspent minute dragged against my intended redemption. And where I watched the clouds or the swaying treetops or whatever excuse the window provided to daydream myself away from Professor Claybay's condescending double index-finger drumrolls against the edge of his scarred and ancient podium.

I'd taken an instant dislike to the guy, fortyish and doughy in the jowls like someone who'd never once imagined owning a souped-up shiny black Camaro or Chevelle and driving it hard and late into the night. I hated his whole act—the bored, half-stifled smirks, classic asshole all the way. The type you just wanted to smack in the face with a volleyball. Once for every tongue-clucking pause he used to punctuate his contempt for each and every one of us. So I just assumed my same seat in back each day and concentrated on tuning out all the bullshit.

"Are we communicating?" he'd say at least once during each class hour, and he'd call somebody's name, which late on a certain Wednesday afternoon happened to be mine. Maybe I heard him and maybe not. I can't honestly remember. But when his tone turned from exasperated to downright mean-minded and he asked me point-blank if I was present—"In the here and now, yes, you, Mr. Grelling"—I nodded and said nothing back.

But I also did not look away. An ongoing problem I'd had with petty authority. A problem that commenced immediately after my dad's death and never abated, and so I didn't take kindly to the way this guy's eyes stayed locked on mine. Still, had he moved on after making his point I might, in spite of the blood-rush in my ears, have let the incident pass. But instead he said, "Really? Then why don't you hold up your notebook and show us what competent note-taking looks like. What it is you found important enough to jot down during this hour so as not to waste my time."

The next day was Thanksgiving. A long weekend ahead, and all I had to do—the smart move—was to study the scuffed-up geography of my boot toe or duck away for a few seconds under the bill of my baseball cap. Anger, as my dad used to say, was always a mistake in retrospect, always a disappointment. He'd had big plans for me, big dreams for his one and only son to turn the world into a better place. But right there, in the suddenness of all those undefined options disappearing, I slowly pushed myself into a standing position. And in a more or less grammatically correct declarative threat I said, "Push on it, pal, and I'm going to drop-kick an exclamation mark sideways right up your tight, compositional ass. All the way to the dead end of every one of your goddamn pretentious sentences."

He gaped and waited dumbfounded, almost hyperventilating, until I sat back down, and when he spoke again his voice cracked and wavered badly.

"Get out," he said. "Leave this classroom now, and don't you ever return. Trash talk somewhere else because you're all done around here. You, Mr. Grelling, are history."

I raised my balled fist up under my chin, elbow hard on my thigh like I needed some serious time to mull over the implications of what he'd said, and how he'd finally inspired a little wrath with his not so compassionate fire.

Then he ordered me out again. "Your last chance," he said, and I thought, Come on, come at me. But instead we all concentrated on his footfalls, heavy in the hallway as he left to go roust the campus feds.

"Hey, screw him," I said, addressing the whole class, tight-lipped and edgy in their seats. "Really, screw this," and two or three students applauded, though only one young woman named Denise, who hadn't said a word all semester, picked up her books and followed me out to the parking lot. And just stood there, high cheekbones and thick, shiny black hair pulled back; and for a second I imagined her sliding into the passenger seat of my beat-up, last-leg Subaru and the two of us lighting out north all the way to Sault Ste. Marie under that dark and pressing late-November sky.

But I guess she had other plans for the night, a date maybe or dinner with her family, because all she said was, "Thanks. Best lecture of the semester."

I smiled and thought about shaking her hand, though what I really wanted was for her to reach up and brush my cheeks with her fingertips. No such luck, and so I got into my car and watched her walk away, her outline already blurry beyond those first fat smacks of rain on the windshield. Then the wipers slapping hard all the way to the bank, where I closed out my savings account before stopping at my junk-cluttered single-bedroom while Mitchell's mantra about *corners, corners, corners* kept playing in my mind. I knew I'd just wrong-turned one toward somewhere I hadn't intended and might not easily get back from.

Corners and curves, and I thought about how the two of us had slow-dragged that jackknife's freshly honed steel blade in a crescent across our thumbs. And how, pressing them together, we'd pledged to each other, "Blood brothers forever." In a world of so many once-only-and-gones, we had suddenly grown wings. Or so it seemed as we crouched side by side over our handlebars and glided around and around those wide new slick-black cul-de-sacs, baseball cards clothes-pinned to the spokes of our silver Schwinns, our ascendance destined to continue on and on. Always in the late evenings under those gray-green streetlamps that eventually led back to our separate houses, mine with the TV on and the drawn shades blinking a different hue with every single scene change.

This one was about to be major, and I considered giving Mitchell a call, a heads-up on my sudden change of plans. But I guzzled the last couple of cold beers from the fridge instead, and then just looked around. Just stood and looked at where I lived, the empty ravioli cans, the unwashed dishes piled in the sink. And without even shutting the front door, I turned and descended the stairs two and three at a time. Like a burglar, though I sure could never have imagined that years later I'd be accused of exactly that. A thief held at gunpoint by the whimpering, drivel-lipped husband of a woman who swore first to him and then under oath that she had not invited me in.

Caught red-handed, the prosecution argued, and I agreed, by hubby himself, home unexpectedly. And me with my pants down and my dick in the cookie jar. But no ski mask—"I mean, God bless the crazies, but how about we return to planet Earth?"—and no stolen jewelry, and to hear her tell it that night in the bar, she wasn't close to being fucking married. Which I made clear to the judge and suggested from the stand that maybe the cops should have dusted the Trojan for fingerprints, given that she was the one who'd rolled it on and then rolled back the bedcovers. That's when my court-appointed lawyer threw up his hands, and I exited the courtroom innocent of all felony charges but nonetheless in handcuffs to serve two consecutive counts of aggravated contempt.

All part of the bar mirror's dark and smoky past, I thought, my face staring back from behind those tiers of coppery silver bottles as I reclaimed my stool. I was the only customer in the joint, and current circumstances seemed suddenly promising enough to order one last round for myself.

"To you," I said, lifting my glass. A simple toast to maybe being on the brink of something better, and for the first time in a long while I felt grateful to be alive. I toasted Mitchell, and then I toasted my dad. Already I was older than he was when he died. A bad heart or enough bad luck, he used to say, will lead you to an early grave. But when I shut my eyes, I could almost feel the old neighborhood's steady beat before things had even the slightest chance to play out wrong. That's what I wanted again: a world scaled back to fit the innocence of that skinny kid's body I used to live inside. At least until the school of hard knocks did its masterful job of teaching all hope and happiness right out of me, summa cum laude all the way.

The snow continued falling but only lightly into the purple twilight when I stepped outside and followed the bartender's simple directions to the bus depot. A left and then a right across the intersection two blocks up. The massacred Samsonite I carried was the same one my wife Helen had fast-packed in a rare tirade before finally throwing me out and filing for divorce.

Up ahead the bus to Escanaba was already boarding, and those last three twenties and change got me a seat and a neatly folded navy blue blanket. A good-looking, thirty-something single woman to sit beside and cover at the knees and let sleep against my shoulder while the frigid world slid by was a long shot indeed. Nonetheless, I figured this was my chance to dream up some better stories to tell for when I arrived. I stood alone for a moment in the dimly lighted aisle, checking both sides, and then I passed slowly all the way to the back without a whispered word to anyone. And without anyone making eye contact or leaning or reaching out, signaling in any way for me to stop.

Nothing big-city about Escanaba, a 1950s throwback kind of town I liked a lot, and hitchhiking down out of the Upper Peninsula I almost crossed over to the other side of Route 2 and stuck out my thumb going north. But the southbound rides came fast, and a hundred plus feet above the Straits on the Mackinac Bridge in those gusts of dwindling light made reversing course seem like a lousy idea once I touched down on the other side.

I hadn't only been all day on the road but more like lost in a continual time warp. And suddenly there I was standing hungry and light-headed under the streetlamp in front of Mitchell and Michelle's aluminum-sided two-story, 1228 Orchard Street. No lights were on. No car in the driveway or parked on the street, and I considered simply sitting on the front porch stairs until someone arrived.

But it was clear-skied, a too-familiar chill already filling my bones. Nothing like Fargo or Grand Forks, of course, where one February it got so badass arctic I could hear the railroad spikes contract in their ties. Too cold even to snow, and those full eight-hour shifts I'd worked outside in the freight yards had taken their toll.

I rang the doorbell just to be sure, and when nobody answered I tried turning the knob. There was a heavy brass knocker, but I didn't want to make that kind of racket so late and listened instead to the few faint disappearing notes of the wind chimes hanging in the next-door neighbor's tree.

Around back I could see the harvest moon reflected and swirling in the birdbath as I fished out the key and unlocked and opened the back door. The wall switch was right there, but before I could even flick it on I heard somebody whispering. I was certain of it. Two voices back and forth, and I stopped dead in my tracks. I don't remember for how long—well beyond those few interminable seconds it took for my eyes to start to adjust. And when a woman's voice said, "Who's there?" I stayed absolutely still, except for the speeded-up motor of my own deep breathing. I thought I smelled marijuana, but maybe not. "Mitchell, is that you?"

I hesitated, and then I cleared my throat and said, "No. No it's not. It's not Mitchell."

Then the sound of pants sliding on, a zipper riding shut. Followed by another run of fast whispering and what sounded like a slider rolling open, and footsteps slapping across a terrace. Possibly only one set, I wasn't sure, and the slider closing and clicking shut.

"Are you still there?" the voice asked, as if it were me, the intruder, who'd turned tail and fled unseen back into the night. It crossed my mind to do just that, half a dozen crouched strides and forever out of there and gone.

But right then music from a clock radio started playing, Frankie Valli and the Four Seasons; and if the adrenaline weirdness hadn't already hit an all-time high, it sure did when the music stopped abruptly and the woman walking into the room straight at me said, "You're Mitchell's friend, aren't you?"

I didn't like being the one on the defensive, fielding all the questions, and so I said, "Whoa," and before she got any closer I spoke my name at her in the semi-dark.

"That's right. Alden," she said softly, the words measured and gentle-like, as if I'd sleepwalked into the wrong house, a kid again, and she was quietly reassuring me that I'd entered a safe place and everything was all right.

"I rang the doorbell," I said.

"Doesn't work," she said, "and anyway that's not what I'm asking. Why don't you turn on the light?"

The distance between us was maybe four feet, and yet her words seemed to be coming at me from some other dimension, more like a dream, and in it she was doing something with her hand. Something relaxed and slow and silent, though the harder I concentrated, the more her outline wavered and blurred.

"Watch your eyes," I said. Then I hit the switch, and in the sudden flood of the overhead as she stepped forward, I believed the lip balm on her pinky fingertip was intended for me, her full lips already glossed and blowsy and sore looking. Like what happens after long, hard-friction kissing, and we were standing almost close enough for that to have occurred. Not that my mind was processing the possibility, though to have claimed it as an entirely unattractive thought would, I was sure even then, prove false and perhaps, given enough time and distance, even cowardly.

"You're letting in the cold," she said, giving me the quick once-over as she closed the tiny round tin and slid it into the back pocket of her beltless low-rider jeans. Her white T-shirt read, Making It Happen—no bra underneath and her breasts sizable—and I tried not to make that the moment's focus either, the door still slightly ajar behind me.

"Probably I should just leave," I said. "Before Mitchell gets home."

"In precisely forty-five minutes," she said. "He never lets his classes out early. He never surprises me like that. Like you did. Ten-thirty he'll be here. Upbeat and on the dot, so I should go upstairs now to take a shower and dry my hair."

It was shoulder length, a shiny shade of brown I liked, styled I could tell, but falling over one eye until she pushed it back behind her ear. She looked like a woman who, unlike me, had never spent any time standing blank-eyed in unemployment lines, and never would. Her toenails were polished red, and what Mitchell had identified as a twelve-year age discrepancy seemed way out of whack. Without turning a blind eye to numbers, mid-twenties was as high as I was going to get.

She wasn't model-stopping-you-in-your-tracks-to-gawk-at beautiful, but attractive in a healthier, less body-abused sort of way. Dark-eyes. Wide mouth turned down, even when she forced a smile and said, "We'll have to work on the timing, but as long as you're here, I'm

Michelle. Mitchell's wife. He's been looking forward to seeing you."

We shook hands and I closed the door, and right up front I said, "Listen, this is none of my affair," and she said back, "No, it's not. It's mine."

"It's none of my business is what I meant. And since I didn't really see anything anyway, I guess I'm good with that," I said. But I wasn't, not entirely.

She folded her arms and stared wide-eyed at me, a slight flex in her hip that I liked. Then that slow, expressionless, continuous nod as if we'd sealed some secret deal or understanding, which maybe we had.

"I'll show you the guest room," she said. "Then you can just make yourself at home."

That entailed walking through a combination library/entertainment area, where she snapped on a stand-up lamp, weakest power, then picked up two throw pillows from the carpeted floor and tossed them onto a love seat. On the wall, behind glass, a movie poster of King Kong chest-pounding out his primordial rage as death planes squalled into the frame behind him. My all-time, bar none, favorite flick, and I wondered if Mitchell and Michelle owned the video, but I didn't ask.

Instead, I watched her slide a wooden dowel into the slider track and pull the draw chain, and I thought for a disoriented couple of seconds that she was going to start the VCR playing, and maybe project the beam onto the wide, slightly wavering screen of the blinds. But she didn't move. She continued standing there facing away from me, and said, though barely audible, "He means nothing. Nothing to me at all."

I didn't know about the truth of that one way or the other. Or whom she was even referencing, though I assumed it to be the phantom caller who'd momentarily slipped out of the scene. But who in my mind I watched get into his parked car a few blocks distant and sneak farther away into the night, worried maybe, or even terrified, of whoever might show up later swinging a baseball bat against the flat, bruised face of his front door.

"I don't need an explanation," I said.

"Why would you?" she asked. "Men never do."

A theory advanced by other women I'd known on their slow or fast track out of flings or marriages. Helen, for one, and every failed attempt to argue her back ended in that same dead silence love always leaves in its vanishing.

I can't recall what I said then, but Michelle turned and sat down hard on the floor, hands pressed between her thighs, head lowered. Spent, I thought, desperate and scared and why not?

Beside her the numerals on the radio alarm slapped over, four times. A stretch between 9:59 and 10:03 p.m. in which no cars drove by, the silence seeming to widen and settle in around us, until she half-gulped back what sounded like a moan that subsided only slightly after I knelt and held both her shoulders, and resisted only minimally when she leaned in against me.

She could not have been more exposed if she'd been stark naked, and after she pulled away I gathered up her underthings, bra and panties, from the black leather swivel recliner and said, "Here. You might want these out of the way."

It was 10:28 when she left me for the soft whispering of the showerhead. And I imagined not Mitchell's headlights bending around the corner, but rather the twin beams on our identical silver three-speeds. That was the summer we'd sneak out our bedroom windows at a designated time and cruise through the cold air eddies and swirls that always drifted in from the cemetery and the surrounding fields a few hours before midnight. I mean, I could almost hear the intricate reverse click-clicking of our pedals as we'd enter those mysterious, isolated thermal pockets left by the sun. And where we'd sometimes stop, straddling our bikes, and name the few identifiable constellations we knew by their animal names: Swan and Bear and Fox. Then we'd be off again, covering what distance we could up and down that next adjacent street as the whole town dreamed around us.

I retraced my short path back out of the room, my stomach growling, and listened to the drain water swirl down through the pipes. What would Mitchell think? His wife in the shower and some strange, weatherworn drifter in a faded Carhartt and hooded sweatshirt sitting all alone, hands folded on the kitchen table. Like someone waiting to be interrogated. Like someone guilty of pressing secretly with tingly fingertips along the spinal ridge of a beautiful woman as she wept.

The only reason why a guy like me ever took a job, or ever would, is money. I'd started young, full-time blue-collar at seventeen, determined to abide by my dad's edict never to freeload, never to be beholden in that way to anyone. The price, he said, was a guaranteed loss of will and self-respect. He was a man determined by optimism and fairness in all things and, because I was his flesh and blood, it felt good to cash my first paycheck and stock Mitchell and Michelle's home deli with kaiser buns, honey ham, cheese and olives and limes, and a month's supply of freshly ground, high-grade Columbian. Coffee, not weed, though one night Michelle tapped on my door, a joint in tow, and in the home of the other most moral man I'd ever known, I invited her in.

"Merci," I said, before I took my first serious toke in over a year, and sat down next to her at the foot of the unmade double bed. She was still wearing the dress she'd worn to work, and the way she crossed and uncrossed her legs, I could see the soft white skin on the backs of her knees. Nothing happened except that we got good and stoned. Got quiet and loud, and I was asleep by the time Mitchell arrived back from teaching his three-hour honors seminar called Situational Ethics. About the fourth time I woke that night, sweaty and dry-mouthed and sitting bolt upright in the predawn darkness, I resolved—just to be on the safe side—to steer clear of the dope and the bourbon whenever Michelle and I were together alone.

She never mentioned her lover, if that was ever even the proper determination. Never once rounded on him or on the subject of her infidelity, acting as if I'd discovered her three weeks earlier locked instead in the arms of her husband as they watched a film together. One night each week, Mitchell would make a ritual stop at Blockbuster on his way home from work. Always Michelle's selection, though I never once heard him gripe about her picks, and so assumed their tastes to be one and the same. Never anything Hollywood, and I came close on a couple of occasions to recommending *King Kong* or *Star Trek* or *Bride of Frankenstein* just for a change of pace.

Mitchell's French was, as he put it, passable. So I alone sat reading the subtitles, and reminding myself all over again why I had never been a serious watcher of foreign films. Not even Sin City stuff, though I admit to pressing the pause and replay button on a particular frame or two in my day. But never anything that charged me in the way Fay Wray's dress hem always did, sliding thighward as she reclined in the fleshy black cave of King Kong's muscled palm.

Which is simply to say that *Un homme et une femme* was doing nothing to keep me awake or entertained. It was Saturday night, I'd put in a long week cutting Christmas trees, and I figured Jean-Louis somebody or other could unzip the leading lady's sleeveless dress without me being there to cheer them on. Yet I stayed right to the end, as I always did, not so much to be polite as to see Michelle lean her head back and to the side and kiss Mitchell on the lips while the credits rolled. A kiss orchestrated, I surmised, for my benefit and mine alone.

That's the image that continued to loop around and around inside my head as I toppled blue spruce and Fraser firs at Londrico's tree farm. Mitchell would drop me off each morning, driving several miles out of his way, my lunch box and his briefcase between us on the seat. He a tenured professor dressed to a T; me in Pac boots, Carhartt jacket, and bibs. In the glaring clash of our separate work-world attire, we looked our age, the years, as he said, dating us by everything youthful that they'd stolen away.

He talked like that, softly, in metaphor, and read poetry and philosophy and listened to books on tape. Except when I was along, and he'd crank up Springsteen just like old times minus the new Ford Taurus and the gray invading our hair. Mutt and Jeff dullards we might have scorned two decades before, has-beens attempting to sing those booze-whipped lyrics we loved all the way back into prime time.

It felt good, though, cruising and hand-tapping the beat against our thighs, Mitchell's raspy, out-of-range, single-note falsetto just bad enough to excite in me that same old road desire to light out half in the bag, never to return home again. In my absence the area had changed so dramatically that I hardly recognized entire parts of it, the gated lakeshore communities, and the upscale downtown with its gas lanterns and cobblestone sidewalks and espresso bars. A whole lot of what I imagined before I arrived back had, from my perspective, been bargained away, and reasons to stick around much beyond the holidays were hard to come by. I'd be unemployed again by then anyway, and that did not cause me to lose one second's sleep.

Still, I liked looking down the empty tree rows, flatbeds from Georgia and the Carolinas being loaded at the snowy field's edge. It was the kind of work that Mitchell and I might have teamed on together as high school kids but never did.

"Pick you up around five," he said. It was Monday, the engine running and the car in park, and the two of us staring out the windshield, the sky salmon-colored above the wave of green-and-white-tipped spires. Another day, I thought, of sunshine and stretches of snow, weather unable to make up its mind.

I got paid by the stump, but I was in no hurry that morning to hit it hard, and might well have gone into the shed to turn on the beat-up space heater, and slow-sip another cup of coffee before putting on my gloves and safety goggles and starting the chain saw. I had the padlock key in my possession since I was the only cutter working that particular eighty all week, which I liked.

"You bet. Five sounds perfect. I'll meet you right here," I said, and got out of the car and leaned back in as I always did and told him, "Teach 'em up, Doc." But he didn't smile, didn't register in any manner at all. Just nodded, the music off, and I said, "Mitchell, you okay?"

Which he'd appeared to be at breakfast, and on the ride over as well but for sure not anymore. He seemed lost somewhere in thought, and I figured that thought's subject might be female, and that I had not in my silence adequately covered his back as I'd always done before, no matter the circumstances.

"He was there at the house, wasn't he?" Mitchell asked, not looking at me, and I said, "Who?"

"It's a straightforward question," he said, without raising his voice. "Either you know what I'm talking about, Alden, or you don't."

He leaned back in the seat, arms out straight and his knuckles bone white on the steering wheel, like he intended to crush the accelerator and fishtail up the double-stump row and come barreling out on the far side of the plantation. He stayed right there, saying nothing else, patient in a way I'd always envied and had long ago identified as the complete opposite of me.

It wasn't hard to figure what he inferred when I hesitated for a few long seconds, then shut the car door and turned away and unlocked the shed and stepped back out a few minutes later, chain saw in hand. The car was still there idling, but I did not acknowledge Mitchell's presence, or gesture in any way in his direction. I simply opened the choke full until the spark plug fired on the fourth or fifth pull, and I squeezed the trigger hard. The two-stroke screamed until I backed off and inserted my earplugs to muffle that awful high-decibel whine, and then I slowly walked out into the trees.

With every tank of gas I'd stop and file and tighten the chain, and at one point, cutting my way back down the spruce row, I did look between the trimmed boughs to see that Mitchell had driven away. The morning had turned to flurries, the temperature falling fast, and my knees had started to lock; my fingers were blistered and going numb in my gloves. The bite of the wind out of the north went right through me. But I stayed at it until late afternoon with only a short lunch break, determined to finish strong on my last day. I hadn't planned on cashing out on such short notice, though in my mind hitching a ride south with the last of the haulers didn't sound bad. Free transportation in exchange for helping them unload, wherever that might be. Savannah, Charleston, somewhere out of the cold.

If I concentrated I could just barely hear their diesels idling on the far side of the much larger adjacent tract, and I might even have started in that direction when Mitchell pulled up by the shed. It wasn't close to full dark yet, but his headlights were on, and the snow slanting through that muted double tunnel of the low beams took on a whiteness that was almost blue. Like the thin frozen rim of the moon some nights, I thought. I could see his silhouette as he stood, and the tiny rising clouds of his breath.

It was one of those intervals when any number of outcomes appeared possible, none of them happy. And I wouldn't have faulted Mitchell if he'd opened the trunk, heaved my bulky suitcase in my direction, and driven away. Almost nothing would have surprised me.

Except, of course, the thing he did, which was to nod and breathe in deeply the sweet, thick scent of all those freshly cut evergreens, and then walk, still dressed in a tie and coat and wingtips, right by me without uttering a word. He took his time but not a long time before hauling one of the bigger blue spruces back to the car and, without him asking, I helped tie it to the roof. Just that morning I'd offered Mitchell and Michelle a free tree; she, more than he, appeared eager to get out the ornaments and put it up early for once.

Mitchell's family always had a Lionel circling under the base of theirs, and bubbler lights and lots of tinsel hanging down, and after my dad died I spent every Christmas Eve and Christmas over there—a second son, as Mitchell's dad used to call me. I even had my own stocking, with "Alden" scripted down its candy-striped length, hanging from their mantel. That's what I remembered as we drove to Meadowbrook, the nursing home and assisted-care facility where Mitchell's parents, both in their mid-eighties, now resided. He said that their lives there were not unpleasant: a conscientious staff, round-the-clock care. That he stopped by afternoons on his free hours, at least every other day. He said, and without rebuke, that Michelle refused to visit, retreating as far away as possible from what lurked just beyond the lightfall. He made even that sound poetic, as if such an admission were in no way incompatible with his ability to love and be protective of the person she was. I wondered if his parents asked about her and, if they did, what he said to them.

I didn't know the nursing home, but the landscape of certain streets along the way there seemed familiar. A few wreaths already on the doors of houses, and one giant Santa attached to somebody's chimney, like he was trying to keep warm, huddled under the huge emptiness of the sky. No stars anywhere and not one word from either of us about what he'd asked me earlier, though had it come up again I would have answered yes. I would have told him that I was sorry.

But it was Mitchell who apologized. "I should have told you," he said. "It wasn't fair to let you walk blind right into the middle of all this."

"The marriage, you mean?"

"It's been on the rocks for a long time," he said, "and there's nothing left to do but give it up. Just let it go. We thought early on," he said, but he didn't finish. Instead he looked over at me, and his face in the headlights of the oncoming car seemed both old and young at the same time, and very tired. "And my parents. Jesus Christ, Alden. Celebrating their sixtieth on New Year's Eve. Imagine," he said. "Sixty years with the same person."

He'd been married fewer than eight, and wedlock for me had been a brief six months. I'd been close to no one for so long that sometimes I'd delude myself into believing it a privacy I'd come to by choice.

"Your mom?" Mitchell asked.

"Nope," I said, and shrugged. "Don't know." And that seemed like explanation enough as we pulled up in front of a large, well-lighted three-story brick building, the walkway shoveled and someone standing by the double doors, smoking a cigarette. Clearly there was a festive event going on inside, and that event, as we entered, included a piano player whose rendition of "Mack the Knife" wasn't half-bad. A tune my dad had liked and sometimes hummed. Had he been among those gathered, he would have gotten up off the couch to welcome us and assist in the tree's accurate alignment in its stand.

But it was Mitchell's folks who came over. They were all dressed up in formal evening attire, and he shook his dad's hand and kissed his mom on her cheek. She seemed not to notice, concentrating instead on me on my back as I reached under the bottom branches to adjust the three screw-in braces. Even upside down I'd recognized her immediately, silver haired and eyes as wide as portals, dark and smart like Mitchell's.

"You remember Alden, Mom," Mitchell said. "From over on Keefe Avenue? He's back visiting. He's been away a long time."

I waved up at her from out of that past, a dislocation far too removed for such on-the-spot recall. I wanted to tell her that I had trouble some nights, too, my own face in the bathroom mirror only vaguely familiar. But Mr. Yates stepped forward then and tapped my boot sole with his cane, his shoulders stooped as he studied me for maybe a full thirty seconds. "Yes," he said. "Yes, indeed. You were always such a nice, polite kid. You always liked to help us out. I remember that. Look," he said to a much younger woman who was suddenly there by his elbow, "he hasn't changed one bit."

"I see that," she said, and smiled at me as she handed him a clear plastic glass half-filled with something bubbly and golden like champagne. "*Salud*," he said, and took a sip, and the woman turned toward Mitchell's mom, who was still standing there tightly clutching her purse.

"Las Vegas," Mitchell's mom said. "The Sands."

The woman nodded reassuringly and pointed over at the piano player, as if to interpret for me, and then she put her arm around Mrs. Yates's shoulder and sang along: "*Danke schoen*, darling, *danke schoen* / Thank you for walks down Lovers Lane."

And right there in the shadow of the newly erected tree, in the angle of the light as I stood up, in the slight shifts of sorrow brought on by the kindness of their voices in flight, I stepped toward that woman, and when the song ended I addressed her by name.

"Denise?" I said, the dimmest glimmer of recognition slowly taking hold in her eyes. I remember swallowing hard, nervously wetting my lips, and Mrs. Yates pointing toward the small ceiling speaker and saying, "Wayne Newton. He's a real heartbreaker," and Mitchell asking, "You two know each other?"

"During our college days of arrested development," I said, and Denise smiled at that, her eyes still on me.

"More like a martial arts class," she said. "You were great, though. You said the right things. You were the brilliant one, Mr. Grelling. On that day anyway. How could I ever forget that?"

For a second the room went quiet, and I thought about how that brief tirade had changed my life forever and not necessarily in the finest ways. I wanted to tell her that she should have come with me. That I would have taught her how to open and close that passenger-side window with a pair of rusted vice grips, and that we might have ended up on a beach somewhere in the warm sun of Mexico. An unlikely but not impossible summary of what might have been us for a while.

The piano player started in again, Andy Williams this time, "Sail Along Silvery Moon." I looked his way and I could see, beyond the white lace curtains framing the window, snow falling again. Against that backdrop a single elderly couple danced cheek to cheek, holding each other close, lost somewhere deep inside their own private radiance. Mitchell had already palmed his mom's elbow and was leading her out there, her hair shining under the cut-glass chandelier.

"May I?" Mr. Yates asked, his hand held out to Denise, who grinned and curtsied and did not glance back at me. Which was, I suppose, at least in part why I ushered myself outside, my jacket zipped against the late-evening swirls and gusts. From where I positioned myself, just beyond the rim the light cast out, the music was no more than a distant thrum.

Another town, another time, I might have been a complete stranger stopping to watch for a moment those diaphanous human shapes floating slowly by like ghosts. Sons and mothers, husbands and wives, and one still dark-haired caregiver who'd followed me just far enough one day to link me to her past. Not that I knew a single intimate thing about her, or ever would. But she was dancing with my best friend's father, and that was the way the world looked. A lot like the snow globe that my dad used to shake and put down in front of me when I was a little kid in love with the silent watching of the objects gone white. A tiny, trance-like galaxy into which I'd stare and stare until whatever had perished magically reappeared. A few rabbits, and a Christmas bear feeding bright red apples to a spotted deer.

Outside the nursing home the snow fell faster. Fell thick until all I could see were my own hands reaching up to pull the sweatshirt hood over my head. Like my dad used to do for me from behind, tying the drawstrings before we'd start downhill on the sled, the runners waxed, and Mitchell with his arms around me, and my dad on the far back leaning hard and steering us with the taut muscles of his thighs, as though the wind were trying to strip the moment away.

But there it was, my dad dead almost thirty years, now back, and my one and only friend dancing with his mom, who might not even have known his name. Or the name of that handsome older man with his arm around a slender, smiling woman half his age. Some bemused god with an odd flair for the holy, I thought, the window amber-lit, and me with my head bowed against a sudden gust, my breathing even and slow. No traffic. And when I closed my eyes I felt, if not anointed, then content. That for sure. And yes, perhaps even grateful for whatever next thing might begin.

[After Everyone Else Has Left]

DOYLE LAIDLAW HAS NEVER attended an execution, has never, one way or another, asserted a conviction—pro or con—concerning capital punishment. He is an ex-husband and the father, still, of one daughter. That daughter, Ellie Laidlaw, is the reason, thirteen years after her disappearance, that he is, at this moment, sitting here behind the closed screen.

It seems another lifetime since he has accepted an invitation anywhere, and he has requested to be seated hours early, though he is not sure why. He is all alone, front row center, dressed casually, wearing sensible shoes and khaki slacks, no coat or tie, attired, perhaps, as he might be to view a Sunday matinee.

He is travel-weary and uncharacteristically unshaven, and, within seconds of closing his eyes, images begin to unreel slow-motion behind his eyelids: a receding tide, a tidal cove gone to mud, and a girl in a bright pink bathing suit and clamming boots crossing that hundred or so yards to the island where, as she's been told repeatedly, she must not go by herself.

"Nuh-uh," she says. "It's *not* dangerous." But Doyle and his wife Francine are adamant worriers, a condition, they concur, that is symptomatic of middle-aged, single-child parents whose absolution has come in what they refer to as their late-stage miracle of conception, this blond girl they worship and love. She is their consciousness, and they will escort her, they promise, across on tomorrow morning's outgoing tide, in search of starfish and horseshoe crabs and those translucent blue mussel shells she sometimes holds up to the sunlight and smiles at. "Okay. Cross your hearts," she says, and in unison they do.

Ellie has, earlier this month, July, turned ten, the evening air warm and still, and Doyle Laidlaw has, with a dull orange pruning saw he found hanging in the unlocked tool shed, just finished butchering two two-by-fours into stubby blocks of kindling. He is yawning, coming, by degrees, fully awake. Francine has driven inland to the Burnt Cove grocery store for the hot dogs and buns and dill pickles he was supposed to have picked up earlier but forgot, and his counterargument of silence, his only defense, he knows now, here in the stark, whitewashed world of this observation room, is nothing less than an admission of guilt.

The rustic cottage he has rented on the coast for the week seems suddenly to tilt and spin again as he stands alone by the unlit fire pit, staring out at the shimmering horizon of panoramic ocean, those thousands and thousands of brightly colored buoys nearly blinding him, and he listens, as always, to that distant, low-guttural echo of what he believes to be a single lobster boat motoring toward the Stonington harbor. It's all there in the police report, his brief nap in the hammock, twenty-five minutes truant is all, tops, a dreamless sleep, a mere doze, though he dreams nightly the opposite of every sworn statement he has ever made in his life, every whispered, guilt-ridden prayer of the non-believer, every angry, self-incriminating arrogation.

Sometimes half a day will go by, an elongated evening maybe, when Doyle Laidlaw quiets his thoughts and forgets that drive from northern Michigan to Maine. Maps and the *Rand McNally Road Atlas* and guide books, those spontaneous family sing-alongs, and how, after arriving, the weather stayed indisputably perfect. Early afternoon breezes, and cadmium-blue sky, and stargazing nights so spectacular that Francine is, right now, holding her daughter's thin index finger and pointing into that immensity while enunciating clearly the syllables of stars, the mythic names of constellations. "Cassiopeia. Venus. Orion," she says, his bow full drawn into an arc of silver light.

And, in Doyle's mind, the lead detective jotting down every detail, his scratchpad filling in shorthand, laser-like, though he is alarmingly nonchalant, careful not to insinuate anything with his questions or his momentary descents into wordlessness, his casual, faraway stares. He is young, late thirties, concentrated more than cold, and Doyle can see out the newly installed bay window behind him how the shallow-chop tide reversing itself has already risen. Half a dozen deputies are wading crotch-deep in a semicircle toward him, silhouetted against the streaky sky, heads lowered as if searching for a body that might float by any second, mere inches below that purple-black surface.

The physical evidence is scant. Someone has found a dragonfly-blue barrette, someone a patch of moss torn up among the tiny scarlet hearts of reindeer lichen. But no weapon or blood-spotted leaves or fern stalks, no handwritten ransom note jackknifed to the trunk of a tree, no blond swatch or lock of angel hair. No semen. And of course no assailant, because in the multiple scenarios of murder and rape and abduction, there is always a getaway boat involved, anchored or stashed on the backside of Pickberry Island, which is otherwise uninhabited and small, all thick growth and shadow, one of a hundred or more scattered across Penobscot Bay.

Never, over the ensuing years, a single suspect or even a distant lead. Until now, which is why Doyle has awakened early this morning in Texas, where he has never before been, to come finally face-to-face with one Clifford Lee Valentine, who has been convicted in another similar crime. And who is scheduled to die at one minute past midnight, all appeals exhausted. He has confessed just one week ago not only to Ellie's murder but to two others, one in Rhode Island and the other in Connecticut. A plumber by trade, unemployed, a drifter at the time of his arrest in the spring of 1985, the only son of a father who, as the court records show, routinely branded him with cigarettes, the pocked scars cratered down the backs of his arms and legs.

Cruel, Doyle thinks, and yet without remorse—in at least a thousand versions of the same recurring dream, he inserts the lethal injection needle directly into this man's heart, this killer of kids who might even have paused, not side-eyed but straight on, to watch Doyle sleep. Who might, in fact, have nodded or smirked as he passed close enough to hear Doyle's open-mouthed breathing, head slightly cocked late on a quiet, laid-back Thursday afternoon. No cooler of beer beneath the hammock, and no radio playing. Doyle is a non-drinker, non-smoker, a careful planner, a grind-it-out advocate of small, sustainable desires, a lifelong disciple of modest ambitions, which are all he has ever coveted or claimed, and then fled from into what has become the scattered jigsaw of his life.

He has, a second or two ago, imagined Ellie at twenty-three, another fleeting glimpse. All told it's all he ever sees of her, obscured by that same unaltered visage of Francine getting out of the car, a bag of groceries in her arms, purse strap slung over her shoulder. As always, and within a few steps of Doyle she's asking, "Where's Ellie?" and he's saying, "She went with you, didn't she?" and the screen door slapping hard behind them as they check her bedroom, the bathroom, and then the two of them back outside shouting her name, waiting a few panicked seconds, and shouting it again and again in every possible off-angle direction: behind them down the fire road, into the conifer woods on both sides, the fog horn sounding every thirty seconds in the distance.

"Where?" Francine says, her wide-set aquamarine eyes just inches from Doyle's, and she's all bone and fascia and sobbing nonstop, arms upflung, "Where? Where did you see her last? Damn you, where, where, where?"

In the eternal time-lapse of those next frantic seconds, he sees, in the tidal mud, two sets of footprints. Side-by-side small and large tracks, leading only one way away from the cottage, and it is a furious run they make, Francine in flip-flops, he barefoot and out ahead, hands cupped around his mouth as he screams and screams his daughter's name. Erupting up the insides of his bare legs and thighs is something akin to squid ink, an expulsion of some dark and pulverized sea substance that stinks of decay, ashy and cold and wet. He is covered in it, black and doglike, and wild with a terror he has never in his mortal being imagined or felt.

Doyle Laidlaw is a public school teacher, seventh-grade geography. A somewhat tragic figure for those familiar with his past, though most of his students pity more his thinning hair and fallen arches, and the way he shuffles stiff-jointed, and takes off his glasses using both hands whenever he turns his back on the class to stare for a few minutes out the second-story window, snow coming down harder and harder like millions and millions of tiny moths. He seems then far gone, both lost and absorbed in some computation so oblique that even he can't factor in all the variables, the longitudes and latitudes of evil, the constantly shifting striations of ice-blue light out there in the godless, grotesque, subarctic fields of the Lord.

Midwinter and he has been granted temporary paid leave from his job in order to travel to Huntsville. A guest of the state, and stated this way he believes his students might glimpse him differently in the collective quorum of their twelve-year-old imaginations. They who believe the whole world is theirs for the taking, the oversized classroom globe spinning and spinning first thing each morning beneath their fingertips. But he has said nothing to them, not one word, nor will he, not ever. He is who he is, narrow-chested, crowding sixty, though much, much older in the false dawns of 2:00 and 3:00 a.m. when he wakes shivering and alone, his face opaque and wavering like a jelly-fish in the naked, glowering light of the bathroom mirror. He wonders if Francine, remarried, the stepmother of another daughter and a son, will show, and if she will still recognize him and perhaps sit down close by without any further need for hatefulness or blame.

He has not laid eyes on her in over a decade, her exact whereabouts unknown to him. No letters or phone calls, though sometimes in the deep, uncharted silence of her absence, he believes he can hear the papery mouths of those Maine wasps in the eaves, chewing and chewing, their gray nests protected from the sun and the rain. Yes, the rain, he thinks, which bore down in sheets for a week straight, beginning the day after Ellie disappeared. Downpours flooded the streets and the abandoned granite quarries, the water rising and rising in the blueberry bogs, the steep embankments eroding as if the whole town might spill over into the sea. The number of hooded search party volunteers diminished hourly, without reinforcements arriving, and without any clue or trace of Ellie. Even the bedsheets stayed sodden and clammy. And, in the cramped confines of that fish tank–sized room that Doyle and Francine rented on short notice in the center of town, and where they overstayed—a month in all—they said things too unhealable to ever mollify or retract.

"We've got each other," Doyle said, softly spoken and meant to buoy somehow, but translated by Francine to mean as in "at least," and she said, "Don't you ever threaten me with that. Don't you dare," as if he'd already given up all hope of Ellie's reappearance.

"It's not a threat," he said. "No, please, that's not what I meant." And he says her name again to himself, here on this drizzly gray morning in the Lone Star State. In a whisper, "Francine," her arm extended full length, a shaky index finger pointed at him, and on the verge, he believes, of squeezing the trigger of the only handgun she has ever in her life imagined holding, and for no earthly purpose other than this.

There is a clock, Doyle assumes, in the execution room, the seconds ticking down. He listens with intense concentration but when he leans forward, elbows on his knees, it is another kind of time he recognizes, the automatic whir of the Kodak Instamatic rewinding. Is it he or Francine who extracts the film cartridge and hands it to the detective?

Doyle cannot remember, though the overexposed front-page snapshot of Ellie—"the missing girl"—in the morning's newspaper appears to him again like a ghost child vanishing across those miles and miles of endless ocean, and gone again the instant he flinches and opens his eyes.

The room, he thinks, is warmer, sweat beading on his lower lip, his heavy breathing as thick and watery as a gag reflex each time he imagines reclaiming his daughter's remains. He has appealed by certified letter to Clifford Lee Valentine for a map, a place name, a single identifiable marker in the maze of this murderer's unreliable and, until now, recalcitrant recollections. "The big sugar," as Clifford says, the final missing piece of the puzzle, and he has agreed to lead authorities to each gravesite on the condition that his sentence be commuted to life without parole. Only then will he offer up the missing coordinates. But first a good-faith, up-front carton of Pall Malls, he says, which Doyle has actually packed in his suitcase but left, last minute, on the unmade motel bed where he slept fitfully, if at all. An hour perhaps, two at the most. Outside the prison vigils are already underway. Doyle knows this, having stepped carefully around those few handfuls of bruised, velvety rose petals scattered on the sidewalk by the main gate, the two Judas trees just beyond in full bloom.

Doyle has not yet met the warden, but has talked twice with him on the telephone, the conversations clipped, segmented, played and replayed in Doyle's mind because, off the record, "It's a no-brainer. Clifford Valentine is lying through his teeth. Out-and-out," as the warden insisted. "Just stalling for time and nothing more." He who will lead nobody anywhere, except to his own overdue extermination on the killing table and, strapped in, whatever he has left to say, if anything, to Doyle or to the attendant priest, to the Almighty himself— not a slobbering sob word of it approximate to any truth beyond the tabloids. "Next thing he'll swear his abusive daddy told him to do it in a dream. Listen, we're beyond all that already and on to God, Mr. Laidlaw."

What's left of Doyle's faith resides nowhere in God's making, though no doubt the veiled, blank-eyed mourners outside at midnight will sing hymns to Him, the Father, asking forgiveness and sprinkling holy water while inside a choir of death-row inmates waits dead-silent in their cells.

He thinks not Valentine but Valentino, and that the warden is probably right that it's all an act, a predictable, last-gasp, dead-man-walking kind of con hastily cut and pasted from old news clippings of cases still unsolved. The warden has seen the spectacle played out a hundred times at least, and yet Doyle's hope—fortified against its own nonexistence—lies with this murderer who, in Doyle's blurred, closed-eyed image of him, has just tipped back his face, his pinched lips drawing hard on a cigarette in the holding cell not fifty yards from where Doyle presently sits. He can almost see him, no guards or handcuffs, no leg shackles, because Doyle is *there*, too, blowing out the match he has just struck, Valentine nodding as they size each other up. There is a black plastic ashtray on the table between them, and Valentine is large or small, six feet perhaps. Or, in the ocular rush of this moment already fleeting, an oily five-three or five-four is likely the more accurate version: the timid, cornered predator last seen in Louisiana, and possibly staring out from a wanted poster that Doyle might have passed without notice while checking his mail, as he does once each week, in his small hometown post office.

And here they both are, not quite strangers anymore, and Doyle says what he has imagined saying to this man forever: "I'm her father. Tell me." But what he really means is, "Spare me." Maybe even, "Save me." And Valentine in mock consideration saying, "Sure. Why not?" But just as abruptly, he shucks the routine and leans midway across the table, leering and flicking his ash. It is already late afternoon, and Valentine, pointing at Doyle's wristwatch, says nothing else, not a single additional word as he slowly ticks the crystal with his fingernail.

What Doyle sees when he opens his eyes is a crew-cut guy in a green jumpsuit, a bottle of Windex hanging from his belt loop, and that exaggerated smile that Doyle's students might refer to in their cockiness as pea brain or retard. Is it for Doyle's amusement that he quick draws and squeezes the white plastic trigger, the plate glass dead-centered with a circle of misty liquid blue? Doyle has never seen a window-pane so clean, the white blind behind it still drawn, and the close-up scrutiny with which this fellow inspects his handiwork makes Doyle wonder if he inadvertently smudged it with his lips or forehead. He wonders if victims' families have pounded their fists against the un-breakable glass, or spat on it, or attacked it with the heels of their shoes. He wonders if even a diamond could cut through it, and he can't help but visualize that next quick nozzle spritz as an expensive ex-ploding jewel. No, not lapis but a blue pearl, and Doyle is momentarily delirious in remembrance of how Francine at their wedding wore a whole string of them, the small ceremony held outside, and the clouds not only cumulus but speeding past as bride and groom delivered their vows.

Doyle says nothing and does not return this custodial inmate's ma-niacal grin, if that, in fact, is what he is. Probably harmless enough but so task-careful and slow that Doyle gets up. "Excuse me," he says, as if he's invisible and afraid that the man might sit right down on his lap.

He needs some air, something to eat, a normal late-Saturday after-noon meal at a family diner, where the price of a spaghetti dinner is determined by the number of meatballs. That kind of place, a conduit home to the same rear booth at Grady's where he and Francine and Ellie used to go every Friday night, idling John Deeres and Farmalls parked among the cars and pickups. He has not been back there a single time, and he avoids at all costs even driving by it, his mind terrified of trading places with who he was then in the calm, familiar middle years of *that* life.

Outside the sky is colorless, the taxis mustard-yellow, and more people—mostly women—have assembled in groups of *them* or *us*. They are interrogating one another with placards and whistles and oc-casional catcalls, and those shiny black nightsticks the cops keep tap-ping to their palms remind Doyle, oddly, of fat holiday church candles, and altar boys, and in the dense fragrance of burning lavender he breaks into a fervent, stiff-jointed jog toward nowhere but away.

He sits alone on a stone bench in a park, evening coming on, and those two wing-clipped swans remanded to a pond so small they nearly blot it out with their size and whiteness. They could be happy anywhere together, Doyle believes, slender necked, and their heads cocked and touching like mirror reflections of each other right there beyond the ferns and cattails.

He looks away, hands folded, unsure of exactly where he is in proximity to the prison. It could be a mile, two miles distant, a maze away, and he is not soaked completely through but the intermittent drizzle has left him cold and shaking, and even hungrier in his present dislocation, though the very thought of food makes him nauseous. He wonders if Clifford Valentine is this instant eating his last meal and the taste in Doyle's mouth turns acrid. He wipes his lips. He's sure he's going to retch and bends over and dry heaves, his stomach muscles contracting tighter and tighter, and he's on all fours on the uncut wet grass, his eyes squeezed tiny and black, and the corneas burning.

He cannot swallow. To steady himself he rocks slowly back and forth, and each time he deep breathes he feels the heavy weight of his knees, as if a child were riding on his back, although every actual angle from which he might visualize such a moment has long since died. Sighted in this position by anyone passing, Doyle Laidlaw is observed for what he's become, sick and frightened and old, struck down by circumstances so obdurate and enduring that he might never again get up.

But he does finally. He rises to that logical next first step of facing toward, and then walking, in what must be the direction back to the prison, its chain-link, its glittering razor wire. He wouldn't swear to it, but yes, he decides, that *is* after all where he's headed. Not by way of any acknowledged real hope for what passes as *closure*, a word he hates, but in lieu of there being an even darker place into which he'll plummet if he does not see this day through.

Not soccer but Kick the Can. That's what Doyle remembers from his childhood, outside at night in the driveway, waiting for his dad to get home, his mom having multiplied times two or three or four the hour he said he'd be away. Or the consecutive days, sometimes, that seemed to bend into or away from one another. There was the wind that flattened the grass, the rain, the undisclosed locations his dad ran off to again and again, the cowering home, and the weather always worsening. Like this, Doyle thinks. Just like this: the clouds gathering, and the distant rolling thunder, and stronger and stronger gusts, and nothing but endless black above these in-the-ground floodlights shining upward. And downward and sideways, a groundswell of illumination so out of sync with those muted B-flat nothing-held-back blues riffs from a saxophone undulating from somewhere deep inside the prison.

Doyle enters through the main gate and is searched again, but this time wanded and patted down, legs spread, palms open, arms held out. He does not look the same, grass stains on his knees, and his gray hair matted flat to his head, his eyes wild and bloodshot. When asked for the letter of invitation, he slides it from his back pocket and holds it out, folded in half, and then in half again, the soggy creases on the verge of separating when the guard takes and carefully opens it. Then asks for some identification, and Doyle, nodding, hands him instead a wallet snapshot of Ellie. "Here," he says, his mouth twitching. "My daughter." And before he speaks her name he clears his throat and looks away. To the left, and then right, as if posing for a mug shot profile, at which point the guard does recognize him and stands aside to let Doyle pass.

Into the men's room first, where he presses the button on the automatic hand dryer, and presses it again before it even stops, its coils blazing orange. Over and over until the forced hot air is swarming in a funnel around him. Doyle feels like a little kid. He's scared and chilled to the bone, and his nose is running. He's ten or eleven, and yes, he misses his dad something terrible but not that unshakable image of him he suddenly conjures up: carcinogenic cheeks, nose alcohol-pitted and purple, a brain choked stupid by booze. A loner to whom Doyle

bore only the slightest physical resemblance growing up, so it is strik-
ing how much they look alike now in the wavering, shiny chrome
reflection of the nozzle. It's as if in a human blink a switch has been
made, and it is not Doyle but his dad who is standing there sobbing,
already more than thirty years dead.

"Excuse me, are you all right?" a man asks, his forehead so fur-
rowed that his eyebrows almost touch.

Doyle has not heard him enter or step out from where one of the
three beige stall doors hangs partway open. Nor has he heard a toilet
or urinal flush, no water sloshing into the sink. It's as if he's appeared
out of nowhere, dressed in a coat and tie, clean-cut, Caucasian, official-
looking but somehow non-penal. A lawyer for the state perhaps, the
kind of attorney Doyle might have trusted had there ever been a trial,
a jury, a guilty verdict handed down, and justice served not only for
his daughter but for all the daughters gone lost and missing over time.

Yes, time, Doyle thinks. Remove just one minute and that terrible
thing that just missed happening never does. They're a family again,
he and Francine and Ellie. Maybe they return another summer, same
Maine town and cottage, Ellie older and knee-deep in a tide pool,
holding up two starfish like pentagrams, and the gulls screeching
overhead.

"Please," Doyle says, "please," though only to himself, his voice
tremulous and cracking, as if begging forgiveness in the pine-scented
bathroom inside a Texas penitentiary is the reason he's traveled all
this way. He breathes deeply. He sniffles and blows his nose, and when
this person touches Doyle's elbow, he glances away toward the ceiling
lights that dim and then brighten again.

"It's that time," the man says, and, after he leaves, Doyle visualizes
Valentine already en route, counting not the seconds anymore but the
one one-hundredths of. It takes Doyle only a moment to calibrate just
how close he is to watching a person die, be put down, as the warden
said, humanely like a dog or a cat gone suddenly feral in the household.

But even in the name of mercy Doyle hesitates to be seated among the aggrieved, and considers returning to his motel instead, and, in tomorrow's predawn, grabbing a shuttle to the airport, some breakfast there, and once airborne watching the great state of Texas recede forever away. Gone, and Doyle back in the classroom the very next day, his voice a mere drone in the chloroformed mindscape of his students still lost to their weekend.

He turns and walks to the mirror, close-up, and he can feel the dull pulse in his fingertips when he presses them to his cheekbones, which are puffy and bruised.

No, not a mirror but a window, and what he hears when he closes his eyes is the powdery thump of a snowball against the glass. He's in his study just off the kitchen, and he can see Ellie's red scarf and mittens as he looks up from his desk, where he's been grading papers all evening, detailed map drawings of the world attached. Doyle *tap-taps* on the pane with his pen tip. Ellie's laughing and waving, and Francine's face in the flood of sentry lights appears almost golden, her breath blue-white in the cold air and not even their shouts for him to come join them can break this silence.

Nothing can, except the amplified click of his shoes on the corridor tiles. He's late and half running, and by the time he steps inside, the blind has already been opened on the execution chamber. Clifford Lee Valentine is barefoot, strapped down, the cuffs of his green prison-issue pants rolled up just beyond his ankles, as if a major vein has been located down there by where the priest stands, clutching a Bible, head bowed so that Doyle cannot see his face.

But he can see Valentine's chest rise and fall, or fall and rise, the IV already in his forearm, fingers limp. He is clean shaven, his hair dark and thick and parted neatly on the left side, and he does not appear panicked or pained, his eyes unblinking and almost opaque from where Doyle stands motionless at the back of the room. He is surprised by how few onlookers are present. Six, he counts, not including himself, the inmate witness side numbering exactly one, a small, white-haired woman who every few seconds offers Valentine another mute, confirming nod. He acknowledges in no way that Doyle can detect that she is even there, though he does not take his eyes off her.

Standing next to Doyle is the man from the lavatory, pad and pen in hand. Not a lawyer after all, but rather a reporter poised to take down a convicted killer's last statement for a story on crime and dying. But it's the warden's voice coming through the ceiling speakers, flat and formal, mere words he's required by Texas law to recite, and without the slightest hank of pity or hate. The seat that Doyle occupied earlier is empty. He makes no move toward it down the narrow aisle as the warden pauses, then takes a few steps closer and addresses Valentine directly, hovering, staring down at the condemned before offering him in the pin-drop silence his unassailable right to speak.

The priest looks up, coaxes, but when Valentine shakes his head no everything stops, the moment on pause, except for the white-haired woman holding a rosary and pressing the backs of both bead-tangled thumbs to her lips. It takes only four or five quiet strides before Doyle slides in next to her. He can almost feel the fire in her hands, and the thin arc of Valentine's eyes shifting, locking on Doyle now, like two men lost and staring back at each other across an expanding field of snow. A silence so deep that the black wall phone doesn't ring, though the warden slowly lifts the receiver, not to his ear, but rather just picks it up and lowers it back into the cradle, and from somewhere someone starts the solution flowing through the clear plastic tube.

Doyle's lips are dry, his throat constricting, and still he does not turn and flee the scene, Valentine's mouth opening and closing in quick small gasps, and the priest, face upturned, making the sign of the cross. The woman next to Doyle keeps praying, moans so low they remind him of distant trains or the wind through the stunted pines behind his house on those nights when he can't sleep.

He hadn't, before it opened, even noticed the door, but there it is, and a doctor has stepped through, the flat silver globe of his stethoscope already pressed to Valentine's chest, and Doyle's heart thrumming so hard he can feel it in his eardrums. *Ka-doom*, *ka-doom* as the sheet is drawn up over the entire length of Valentine's body, only the toes exposed, and that is the image Doyle holds onto after the viewing room blind is closed. Why he thinks of the slippers beside his bed he hasn't a clue, though maybe to remind himself how often he has sat in the dark, his knees drawn up under the covers, waiting for first light.

Everyone except this woman next to him has left, and when she takes his hand and squeezes tightly, he squeezes back. Not a single word is whispered. They stare straight ahead without expression, the two of them here alone, and more remote in their singleness than any truth he could have possibly, in this human life, ever believed or known.

[Saint Ours]

HERE'S WHAT THE GUY I *don't* live with anymore said: "Charlene, if you could only imagine yourself as a feral, teeth-bearing, timber wolf bitch in heat, then you and me—we'd be a whole lot better suited." His name is Paulie. And when, on our honeymoon, I refused to get down on all fours and snarl and snap and howl back at him, he grabbed me and attempted to force me down onto the wall-to-wall pea-green shag, and I said, "This is grounds for divorce, you know?"

He'd been downing Kamikazes and doing bong hits—which excuses nothing—and I flashed that instant on how our vows had been so entirely misinterpreted, and in my mind already null and void for as long as we both shall live. And that at some undetermined future date I would sign and serve him with walking papers, and skip town well in advance of all the predictable fireworks.

The man whose bed I'm currently sleeping in has no clue that I'm still legally wed or, for that matter, that I ever was. Or that a fifty-fifty split of everything that Paulie and I own jointly wouldn't buy me

fifteen minutes on Dream Street. How I've even gotten this far mysti-
fies, the rust-riddled GMC three-quarter-ton pickup in need of a ring
job and a tread-bearing set of tires, and headlights that don't strobe
or short out on the potholes and washboards and frost heaves. The
truck is in Paulie's name alone and insofar as he is by nature ornery
and vengeful, and because he always reverts to form, he has undoubt-
edly reported the vehicle stolen. Right, some choice he hung on me:
grand theft auto or miraculously grow myself a set of wings for my
unmapped, zigzag getaway to wherever two seventy-five and change
would land me.

Vermont tags, and so when questioned I said, "Montpelier," when
in fact the driveway I slowly backed out of almost two months ago is
just outside of Bellows Falls. Lying is *not* habitual with me, though it
is my theory that any potential love arrangement that can't bear a certain degree of deception was never in the first place meant to be. Not
that love or longing or even a vague yearning was what was at stake.
The plan was simply to hole up, for as long as need be, and attempt to
reset and regain my bearings. No rush or panic and trust me when I
say that any slue-footed P.I. who can track me here is worth his weight
in minks and sables.

"Fair enough, but why Carp Lake of all places?" Grove asked, and
my instinct was to lower the coffeepot onto the Formica tabletop, and
slide right up tight to him on the midnight-blue vinyl of that back
corner-booth seat where he used to sit near closing, and plant a kiss
smack-dab on his lips and whisper, "You. You're the reason." Instead
I said, "Why not?" and poured him another warm-up on the house,
and look where I ended up, safely tucked under an elk hide that must
weigh a full forty pounds, the fur thick and fist-deep and shiny.

Grove claims that there are only three seasons in northern Michigan: July, August, and winter. Endless subantarctic wind chills and
whiteouts, he says, and the county roads impassable for days on end.
No mail, schools shut down, and no place to escape without snowshoes
or a snowmobile, and I thought, Perfect.

A single February, he insists, can last a full year. For some people, half a lifetime, and even in the sack his shiny, dark hair appears wind-swept whenever I wake next to him, his head sometimes sideways on my lower abdomen. Other times in the drowse between sleeping and waking I'll reach into that empty space where, out of habit, I already expect him to be. Then I open my eyes to find him fully clothed and staring down like he's surprised to find me there. His cheeks as red as if he's just stepped inside from the cold outdoors after casting and casting his fly line into those blind, predawn hours of darkness.

Unlike me he's currently unemployed. But in three weeks, he says—on the trout opener—he'll resume guiding again. Just last week he got up and cracked the bedroom window an inch or two so that I could hear the water eddy and flow around that wide sweep in the horseshoe bend just upriver from us. He said, "Hey, Charlene, look," and in the slant of early morning light those two gigantic weeping willows that lean out over the far bank glowed iridescent, like lemons. Right, spring hopes eternal, and yesterday, like magic, the first of the dive-bombing kingfishers arrived.

I've only ever fished with night crawlers or miniature marshmal-lows on a bare hook, with a bell sinker to carry the bait down and out away from the shore. For bullheads or suckers, lazy, good-for-nothing pig-eyed bottom feeders as Darrell, my stepfather at the time, referred to them, and he sure never contemplated paying anyone to lead us anywhere. He wouldn't even tell my mom where we were going. "Our secret spot," he'd say, and no, she couldn't tag along, not then, not ever, and he'd quick-wink over at me. I was thirteen, prime-time jail-bait in skin-fitting Levi cutoffs, my first bra front-hooked and lacy and shiny black. Sometimes on those hot, humid afternoons I'd say to him, "It's no different than a bikini top," and unbutton my shirt and sit there half-unclad while he chain-smoked, his narrow eyes bead-hard on me. Like a garpike's or what I conjured a barracuda's to be. Not so different but even more intense and concentrated than when he tied up a tire swing in our backyard a few years earlier, needing approval from me, as I'd overheard my mom say to him, now that he was going to be my father.

As part of our Just Say No education we'd previewed half a dozen perv films in homeroom, which we referred to as C Block, all gray concrete walls and those heavy, steamy, yeasty-smelling canvas green shades yanked tight to the sills. Although Darrell possessed certain key slimeball tendencies, he never so much as copped a feel or moved on me in any overt physical way. Except for one time to tuck a loose strand of hair behind my ear, and eventually, like my father, he disappeared too, *his* current whereabouts unknown.

Grove is nothing like Darrell or Paulie. Everything neat and tidy, and when I first inquired as to his line of work, he said, "Dining on the fly. Strictly an under-the-table, word-of-mouth operation," and I thought, Okay, fine, but factor in his *Better Homes & Gardens* kitchen, and fancy-ass drift boat, and French wine by the case and it all points to some fatter scratch elsewhere.

Drugs. Reverse alimony. Insurance fraud that I'd heard Paulie and his Saturday afternoon chugalugging buddies gas on about. Working up their slow, predictable fury and daydreaming aloud how just one fucking sweet-deal windfall of a scam would instantly transform them into blue bloods. Kings of the trailer park, as they said. But Grove's cover? "A moderate trust," he said, more question than statement, as if appealing to my imagination to buy into whatever he was selling, but I thought, Say again? As in, get screwed royally more than a time or two and it behooves a woman on the loose to scrutinize the motives of any man. And that includes even a charmer as apparently decent and soft-spoken as Grove.

As if reading my mind he said, "An inheritance." And to corroborate the claim, he showed me the ornate, bowlegged cherrywood leather-top desk on which he ties flies in his shop out back. They're intricate and gorgeous and now and again he'll hold one out to me in the shallow pool of his palm and whisper its Latin name: *Isonychia,* he'll say. *Hexagenia limbata. Ephemerella dorothea.*

In grade school I sat for a while in the second row of desks next to a boy from Brazil, whose name I can't anymore recall, and whose seat, one day, went unoccupied, and stayed that way for the remainder of the school year. Olive skin, eyes oval and dark brown like fresh roasted almonds, and I swear Grove could be that kid grown up, his teeth even straighter and whiter now, the moist-looking lips, the remote, wry smile. Quite possibly someone who, a few generations removed, might actually have been connected to the ruling class, and whose life out here in the boonies was some oddball remnant of a more glamorous and pedigreed past.

Grove has a college degree in entomology, which explains why he examines so carefully the submerged stones he lifts from the riverbed, turning them over and over in his hands. He makes sketches and takes meticulous notes in his daybooks on what he sees. "Helgramites. Nymphs. Midges. Insect larvae," he says of the water samples he collects in tiny glass tubes literally teeming with invisible protozoa come to life under the intense magnification of his microscope. Incredible, and Holy Mary Mother, if that constitutes scholarship, then maybe higher education is not, after all, as my mom maintained, just another impossible wide-eyed pipe dream. "Listen to me, Miss Cum Laude. Forget about the I.V. Leagues, okay?"

"*Ivy* Leagues," I corrected. "Like on vines and archways and courtyards." And she said back, "Beauty school, Charlene. Go there and call it college if need be. Think hair. Think manicures and blush and mascara," which struck me as unenlightened and small-minded and hopefully untrue.

My teachers all concurred that I was plenty bright enough. A regular fucking brainiac, as Paulie used to describe me. A potential star pupil who loved to read, but nothing by the book, so to speak. Meaning nothing that was ever assigned, but I'd taken the SATs and scored nationally in the ninetieth percentile on the verbal. Somewhere in my old room at my mom's house, I've still got that No. 2 pencil I used to blacken those oblong bubbles.

Grove, naturally, isn't privy to any of this. He never pushes or pries and neither do I, and so, at least in the short term, our hidden private selves are therefore impossible to trace. All secrets aside, what's obvious to both of us is this: That I am all legs, disproportionate as a cricket, and that the hem of my tight-fitting waitress uniform quits a good six inches shy of my knees. I have witnessed men jolted back alive when I've slow-turned and walked away after taking their orders. It's a walk I perfected in front of the full-length mirror behind my closet door, as if my career path had been determined when I was maybe ten or eleven, already a showgirl of sorts in my mom's lilac lipstick and three-inch heels. All prettied up and the mirror two-way, I imagined, and men of all ages huddled up, mouths agape and staring, the sky above the house about to crack wide open, all thunder and rumble and hellfire.

Yes, me, Charlene St. Ours. That's my maiden name, reclaimed, and as my real dad used to say, a name as pure and precious as poured silver. St. Ours, as if a single patron was watching over us, the guardian saint of dreams, he said, except that hardly ever seemed the case, and no doubt goes a long way toward explaining how I hooked up with Paulie in the first place. That and dumb judgment and being bone tired and emptied out by dead-end jobs and fewer and fewer prospects going forward. And Paulie, a misunderstood fellow sufferer, exuded some vague, dense concept of our impending, preordained glory.

My dad believed that the true worth of any life was how well you survived your own worst human share of it, and not how you warded it off, which he contended was impossible so why even try. Arguments I barely understood at ten years old, which is when he left us for good. But all things being unequal, here I am, beaten up and down and sideways, but intact enough at thirty-five to believe, against the odds, that the happier outcome the human heart was meant to act on is still possible, maybe. If that includes toughing it out for tips at the Day-Runner for a while, so be it. I mean—could be it's as simple as this: We do what we do. We let down our hair, lips slightly parted, and undress like those goddesses men believe us to be in the early winter dusk, and sometimes, we want to believe in that image, too.

So yes, I've consciously withheld from Grove any exacting, incriminating personal details. My hapless, head-on, rent-to-own wreck of a marriage, for starters. Paulie either sucking down beers or passed out cold or gone off to the casino in some last ditch to resurrect our bankrupt fortunes.

It's sad but true that I've viewed more of this wide world than I'd like to admit from the tin-hootch roof of a house trailer with cheap venetian blinds and russet-colored dollar-a-yard carpeting. There, in the summer months, Paulie stashes a grill and a Styrofoam cooler of Hamm's on ice. And he refers to the two wooden pallets and makeshift planking that he hauled up there as our—ready for this?—portico. Don't ask me from where in his limited vocabulary he exhumed *that* gem, but I quote: "Charlene. Go ahead and climb that ladder, Princess, and plant your deadfall of a fanny on our frigging, brand-new private portico, for which we owe nobody, not one red goddamn cent."

"Judas Priest" was my initial take as I ascended and sat down on the ripped and battered Naugahyde recliner. The sky blinding and peacock blue above as if Paulie had, in a sudden rush or brainstorm, positioned us that much closer to the Almighty himself, the arc of our lives suddenly all faith and mirth and sunshine and bells.

A eureka moment if ever there was one: this was my future, already rooted out and picked over, the reek of methane in the wrong wind direction wafting in continuous waves from the landfill that abutted us. So pungent sometimes, I wondered why, when Paulie torched a bone or a cigarette, the entire mobile home park didn't instantly incinerate in a single sonic-boom bomb burst of apocalyptic white light.

And so it felt magical when Grove cooked and served *me* that first dinner, an entrée of venison medallions, so tender I had to resist swallowing each bite whole. Followed by flaming crème de something or other for dessert. He's got a stand-up, double-door stainless steel freezer packed with wild game, each vacuum-sealed see-through packet labeled and dated. And a smokehouse out back and half a dozen stump seats arranged around a fire pit to entertain his wilderness-seeking fat-cat clients. He says that he offers them Cutty Sark or cognac. Coffee and sambuca. Hand-wrapped Cuban cigars, which accounts for the humidor, the first I'd ever laid eyes on, and perhaps, in context, a minor eccentricity after all.

There are enough books stacked on the living room shelves to rival my hometown library: *Thinking Like A Mountain*—that's a title that struck a nerve. So I started reading. And ever since, whenever a cloud-bank in a particular shape rolls in, I imagine snowcapped peaks, and canyon passes where a train keeps wending through the switchbacks, a man and a woman meeting by chance for the first time late at night in the dining car. Not entirely unlike Grove and me, not if you blur your vision and ignore the smell of pork ribs, the spat and sizzle of the grill, and those distant, sad howls of coyotes late at night.

I suppose this merely confirms what my dad always said about me: "A dreamer is what you are," as if this constituted a virtue among virtues. "Never lose that, Charlene. Never, ever give it up. Make it all real, it's ruined. Remember—there's always a quiet, unviolated place inside your mind somewhere. Find it and go there," he said, "no matter what." As if by merely closing my eyes I might dispense a few minutes worth of hope and gladness against the world's cruel design to devour alive the entire tribe of have-nots like us.

He worked at the foundry—his face a deep copper color in all seasons. Except for around his eyes; the infernal lava-like boil and swirl of the forges impossible to look into without double-ply, black-lensed safety goggles. Often his lips got so badly blistered he'd press them ever so lightly to his boiler suit sleeve before kissing my mom. I don't know why but I intuited that moment of pain as true love, which it turned out over time not to be, and so I remain thankful that they never hazarded any other offspring. Ditto for me, at least so far. That, too, got to be an issue with Paulie, who, because we hadn't yet—his exact phrasing again—"made us a little monkey," accused me of secretly using birth control. For the public record, I did, and do, distributed free at the county health clinic.

Grove and I have been together for exactly twenty-two days and nobody here is laying claim or talking long-term anything, and no mention whatsoever of where the potential holy mess that great sex between complete strangers can sometimes lead. Ask my dad, who left with a woman half his age and whom my mom still refers to as "that little zip of a slut with the tight ass and the high-rise plastic tits." He promised support payments but nothing legally deeded and so you can figure in two seconds flat the upshot of that.

"Why?" Grove asked the first time he pulled up at the unnamed, slashed-rate four-unit hovel of a motel. Whitewashed plasterboard walls and ceiling, a stubby pull-chain and a forty-watt bare light bulb. One dinky window beside the hollow-core front door, where I'd been slumming, broke and depressed and convinced that I'd run through my life savings only to end up in a dive more dismal and claustrophobic than our faded pink coffin of a house trailer. No phone or TV, and someone's abandoned black slip still hanging on a single dowel in the tiniest closet I'd ever seen. And to top it off, a mattress that smelled like straw and dried pee.

"Because it's all I can afford for now," I told him.

"No better than sheep sheds nailed together," he said. "That's all they are. And I don't intend to intrude on your personal space, but hey, listen. This is no place for a person to try and survive for more than a night or two."

That's when he offered to let me crash at his cabin until I got back on my feet, and to his invitation I all but broke down sobbing, Yes. No set timetable, he said, and rent-free, and best of all no questions asked. Plus all the high-ticket cuisine that my growling, flat, on-the-run stomach desired. Once every two months he drives south all the way to Traverse City to stock up, and when we sat down to that first candlelit dinner I could name maybe half of what I was lifting to my mouth.

"Y'know of course," Gina, the owner of the Day-Runner, says, and pauses, and I think, No, I honest to God don't, but it doesn't matter one way or the other because here we go again. Round and round on another after-hours speed trap check-in of my misinformed emotions. "Women end up alone and snowbound here's what happens first thing," she says. "They go stupid, and then downright loony. Get a glimpse of Grove a few days grizzled and it's no secret that he's been down and around that proverbial bend more than a time or two."

"Maybe I get the vapors for older boatmen," I say. "And who's snowbound anymore? I can hightail out of here anytime, if and when I choose." What I keep to myself is that the thought *has* seized hold more and more with every passing night, my few belongings stuffed in a pillowcase and already in the pickup.

Gina just nods and takes a deep, slow drag, the doors to both restrooms propped open and the undiluted smell of industrial-grade toilet bowl cleaner thicker than the smoke of her cigarette. Which, in the neon of the house lights dimmed down, turns a pale, murky, eerie green when she exhales slow-motion through her nostrils and mouth.

It's almost the witching hour and we're the only ones in the restaurant, having wiped down counters and tabletops, vacuumed, refilled the ketchups. Marking time, as Gina, the native martyr who's never in any hurry to leave, says. Yeah, sit long enough and time gets earlier is her take, but I don't buy into a single disappearing second of it. She's got two out-of-the house kids, a daughter and a son. Long goners, as she calls them, off and running from one mess to another. And, God forbid, no man onsite or lurking anywhere on the shadowy periphery. Precisely the way she prefers it, without any hassles or obligations "to love and cherish," which, as she says, is what all that commitment bullshit inevitably turns out to be.

Her feet are propped up on the opposite booth seat, right next to me, the soles of her shoes gum rubber, her ankles plumped-out and veiny. Her eyes, too, all glassy and half-lidded in their sockets, and I envision if she were to close them that she'd nod instantly off, and wake and rise minutes before first light to start the coffee brewing again, her seventh consecutive double shift this week. A menu that never changes and that I memorized in less than fifteen minutes so I could clock through the routine with my mind leaping ahead toward other things. Like the new moon, and the next time it's full, Grove promises—weather permitting—that he'll slow-float me downriver so I can observe the swirls of monster brown trout turned carnivorous and rising for injured bats or mice or voles. He ties those, too, with deer hair and hackle, their eyes sad and oversized, and their tiny pointed ears so soft and real-looking I want to carry them into a field miles removed from any waterway and let them go.

"It's all illusion," Gina says, and points through the thick plate-glass window to the twenty-four-hour 7-Eleven across the street lighted up like a mackerel sky. "Even the First Lady at this hour is as ordinary and tragic as the rest of us. At this hour, Charlene, *every*body's heart hurts. Present company no exception, and don't pretend otherwise or you wouldn't be sitting here in the first place."

The smoke rings she blows widen and break around me like the outlines of mottled, oval green mirrors, and for a few seconds I'm staring not at Gina but at my own face, ghostlike and reflected back in the sudden time warp of twenty years.

Gina says, "Excuse me, but I'm confused. Now tell me again what it is you're going to miss most on your way out? *If* and when you go."

Attitude aside, Gina's okay, but Venus flytrap all the way when it comes to late-night one-on-ones, where she's forever throwing down on me like this with questions and innuendo calculated pretty much to tick me off. Never one moment's tired silence to offset the running commentary. Like my mom at her nosiest sleuthing-around worst used to do. "Just wait, you'll see," but what I need is to get *gone* from here, where I've force-smiled and small-talked and balanced overloaded trays until my arms and jaw and brain waves ached. Odds are that Grove will be awake, the woodstove aglow, like always, and the elk hide folded back on the king-size goose-down mattress. Feathers below, pelts above, but I don't want to confide or bitch-snipe another opening for Gina to crawl through and prolong the conversation.

"The way he washes and hand-dries and stacks the dishes. That's what I'll miss most," I say, as if Grove were the busboy I split tips with. The one who is nineteen and married and hitchhikes to work and back. A father already, another child on the way. A sweet, sweet-faced kid who, first thing after taking off his coat and hat, folds a white dishtowel lengthwise and drapes it over his left shoulder. Like he's about to back-step away from the scalding trough of the soak sink and instead burp and rock an infant right there, in the rising steam and clot of the kitchen.

His wife, who I've met one time only, bears a fair likeness to the babysitter my mom used to hire to watch me whenever my father stormed out, where to or for how long we never knew. In his absence my mom would sit alone, oftentimes for hours, in her Cutlass Supreme, parked in our driveway of spurge and flowering, impossible-to-kill, spiky yellow weeds. Always in that same sleeveless dress, open-backed and low cut with all the wrong kind of cleavage. Even her fake eyelashes and earrings drooped too low, as if her entire wardrobe was a fashion statement about gravity and early middle age and being suddenly single again and with nowhere to go. Only her teased dark strands spiraled upward from their roots into a hair-sprayed beehive of sticky platinum blonde.

She'd start the engine and a few seconds later shut it off. Take another belt of Bacardi straight from the pint bottle and chain smoke, the dome light on and then off and the tail fire of her cigarette butts arcing out into the blacked-up night like a spray of tiny meteors. I'd watch from the living room window, waving every ten or so minutes to try and summon her back inside, her entire body doing that shuddery thing that meant she was crying big time again. And my dad's cryptic parting words to us on his way out a couple months earlier? "She'll adapt," he'd said about me. "Both of you will, just give it time." But no place inside me ever came close to accommodating his absence or my mom's chronic and forever deepening despair. "No, not a divorce, an annulment," she said. "Do you even understand what he's asking for, Charlene? What the word means? That we never happened. Never were. Not for one crummy, disappearing day of our lives together did any of this matter. So cruel," she said. "So goddamn godless and beyond belief pitiful and downright cruel. And what did we ever do to deserve this? What?" she said, as if I might on the spot hatch some fairy-tale scheme that would somehow make her lonely, self-loathing life a tad bit easier. No kidding, I should have taken a vow right then and there to never, ever marry or fall in love.

"Mm-hmm. Feature that," Gina says, and instead of stubbing out her Parliament in the plastic ashtray, she stands the cigarette on end on the tabletop between us, like a fat blown-out birthday candle. "Knocks himself out on the domestic front, does he?"

"That's him all over," I say. "Times ten." And I flutter my eyelashes and without another word I grab my coat and scarf and long-stride out into the rear parking lot, the spare front door key to the cabin in my apron pocket. Along with my paycheck and a folded in half paper-clipped wad of maybe fifty tip bucks, not a single crisp, recently minted bill among them. Wages only livable under the ongoing arrangement, whereby I spring for pretty much nothing other than my own gasoline and cell phone. And those few privacy items for "the lady of the cabin," as Gina has taken to calling me.

Never *to* her but in large measure, I admit that she's not entirely mistaken. I am, for better or worse, a kept woman, living, for a change, free of repossessors and delinquent bills, and monthly phone threats to cut off the heat and electricity. Under those circumstances name me one woman who wouldn't have deferred a history that resembles in any way where I've come from? Grove's not only content with our arrangement, but determined, not to amend a single thing. Some part of me wishes he would, although I guess the ban on heavy lifting those hidden mangles and menaces of our concealed histories still stands. Two nights ago I inadvertently mentioned *x* or *y*—don't ask me what, I sure wasn't consciously revealing any hard-luck misadventure of who I was—and Grove interrupted mid-sentence, silently pressing his index finger to his lips, and slow-shaking his head from side to side. Reminding me once again that we existed aware of each other not in the moment gone or about to be, but rather fixed in the continuous present moment only, unaware of any shared or separate past translating into a future *we* or *us*.

So I just nodded and lay back down. Because we were already in bed, I faked an orgasm at the first touch of his tongue. "Yes," he whispered. Meaning, Darling-Heart, Starlet Lover—that mystery woman I used to imagine fulfilling forever every man's wildest dream-fantasies and desires.

Tonight is cold but no snow and there are glittering constellations galore, an intermittent flare pulsing beyond the trees. So far so good, I guess. After all, the engine turns over and catches on the first try. The idle rough, plus a flaming acetylene-blue backfire or two, but when I hit the light switch even that row of orange operas on the front lip of the cab blinks on. Grove has rewired the pickup from beezer to back end, a phrase I liked and hooted at when he first used it. He's also replaced the four baldies with retreads from the auto pound, as if they, too, had been free-for-the-adopting discards caged right along with all the lost or runaway or cast-off kitties and pooches.

Included in the emergency survival pack that he assembled for me is a heavy black billy club of a flashlight that holds six batteries. Plus a couple of Mars bars and a thermal blanket in case of breakdowns, the roads to the cabin mostly two-track and sometimes snow-sealed or choked out by drifts or fallen limbs and no way to turn around. "Yes, by all means, in April. Nobody's home free yet," as Grove continues to tell me, the swollen eyes of winter-kill deer, the delicacy of ravens and crows and those bald, redheaded, hook-beaked, blood-faced turkey vultures, their wings stretched wide against wherever the barren white sky either ends or begins.

He reminds me that a snap freeze can claim your toes or fingertips. I take heed but wish on nights like this that *some*thing like love suddenly discovered superseded the routines of survival: Get safely back and get laid. Go to sleep. Morning coffee together while watching the purple ripples on the river so perfectly tuned but the music dialed down to zero.

Around the moon, a halo of frost, but the windshield is clear and the gas tank nearly full. There's a sign for Good Hart pointing south, and what's left of the snow burns almost incandescent along the ditch line, the trees strung out in silhouette for as far as I can see. "You'll be years getting there," my dad liked to say. "But that's okay." And I'd nod like I understood as he walked straight away from me into the darkness. Where he'd stop finally and light those sparklers he always kept on hand in every season. A ritual he'd perform whenever I asked, and, from that same paced-off distance, he'd dazzle me with crazy-angled loops of fire.

Had Grove in a sudden turn of mind even halfway considered my life worth telling, I might have mentioned that the looping, zigzag wing-light was so bright it turned that part of the field behind our house silver. Like an actual angel was out there dancing under the dome of the sky. I lean forward, and lost somewhere up there in the night swirl is the Lute-Bearer and the Fair Star of the Waters but in what direction I haven't a clue and the pickup at such low speeds tends to stall out anyhow.

I hit the gas and high beams and head in an unknown direction. And this: the double thud of tires across the railroad tracks reminding me of a heartbeat, and so I grip the steering wheel hard against that chronic and violent shimmy as if to hold the pickup from shaking apart. Not until the speedometer's glow-green needle exceeds fifty-five does the world appear quiet and calm again. I crack the window barely an inch. And, for one brief disappearing second before that upcoming first sharp dip in the road, the power lines gleam in the rearview like harp strings.

[This Season of Mercy]

YOUR DAD SPENDS the night in a small-town jail cell for women and believe me, the hang-ups begin, the crank calls, the muffled late-night threats, the sharpshooter's heavy silence. It's possible, dressed like he was on a Saturday night, and the drunk tank most likely occupied, that Deputy Overmyer only meant to protect him. Either that or teach him a lesson, though lessons of that sort were the ones my dad did not easily comprehend.

All I know for certain is that my mom's the one who bailed him out, so I didn't actually see him behind bars, but I was still wide awake when the family pickup pulled into our driveway. By the time the front door lock clicked open and my parents entered the living room, I was already positioned on the couch, pencil and math book firmly in hand. Props to make them believe that I'd stayed up late, determined to solve those nearly impossible story problems that Sister Regina, our eighth-grade teacher, called barometers for measuring our future as failures if we did not brighten up.

At first my parents didn't see me in the half dark, but when my mom twisted the dimmer switch and the ceiling light intensified, they both just stared, my mom's unformed words turning first into hesitant, audible deep breaths before she finally composed herself enough to say, "Henry, as long as you're up to see this, I'd like you to meet your father."

I tensed right tight to that sharp edge in her tone, thinking that my dad might grab hold of something near at hand, like he did that ceramic flower vase a few years back, after he'd tied one on and my mom dressed him down pretty good, and then back up the other side. He didn't heave the vase like I thought he might, his arm half-cocked, but I could sure see that as a possible outcome, the imagined blue and yellow explosions of crockery as loud as shotgun fire against the living room wall.

This time, to my surprise, he just shrugged and smiled, and, for a moment, I believed he might drop the wavy red wig he held, and then reach out to shake my hand like some happy-go-lucky middle-aged cross-dressing interloper. His smeared lipstick was as bright as boiling lava, and he needed a shave, and I knew right away that he'd been drinking and fighting, and that this time my mom's anger would lose out—and most likely already had—to her slow-growing depression and fatigue. She'd been diagnosed two months earlier with Lyme disease, and even her regular customers at Cutz went elsewhere to get their hair done, not wanting to drive this far outside of town to some makeshift beauty salon in our living room, and my mom's joints having already turned arthritic.

"In vino veritas. There's truth in the wine. Isn't that right?" she said to my dad, as she poured herself a full glass of ginger ale, and sniffed its not-so-complicated bouquet, and raised it directly at him. "You," she said. "To you, Frank." And only then did he step forward, taking hold of both her wrists and sipping carefully, and then winking his painful bloodshot wink over at me.

He'd pulled some off-the-wall stunts in the past, but this one put them all to shame, and it wasn't a reach to assume that it would at some point shame him too, and maybe already had. All I could conclude was that the slaughterhouse where he worked had laid him off again, or worse, though I did not at that moment want to consider the possibility. Bad enough they'd already cut back his hours, he'd said, and predicted each night at dinner that it was only a matter of time before they cut him loose for good. Bastards, he'd called them. A bunch of vindictive, northern Michigan canvas slappers.

Which only contributed to my mom's long-standing anthem of college, college, college, what she called trading places, trading up, and she said, "Some education, him seeing you in this condition. Jesus. Go clean yourself up. Take a cold shower, Frank, and a good long look at yourself, and go to bed."

His expression went vacant, but he nodded then in earnest and released his grip. When she turned her face away from his swollen, split-lip kiss to her cheek, the giant tears he mimed seemed to place no end to the potential blend of romance and pathos in our house. They'd gotten almost good at this, for my sake I guess, the two of them acting out the drama of the everyday gone momentarily berserk. But I could see that the effort had finally worn my mom down, and that she was real close to crying.

I was both startled and confused to see my dad like this, but not really all that worried. Or I was, but I'd just turned thirteen, and my dad's bruised and distorted face seemed less pained than it should have been. I mean, even all busted up I could still detect a smug satisfaction, which on TV might actually have passed for a tough-guy sort of charm, though I much preferred him in his white hard hat and steel-toed safety shoes, his normal dad look each morning when he dropped me off at school.

From as far back as I can remember, I was frightened by storms. I hated them, and even though the one predicted was still well out of earshot, I could almost feel its distant gaping rumble, the temperature already starting to fall. And, not all that far behind, those fast-approaching, interminable months of snow, the barn decrepit and roofless but the silo out back still standing, a round crisscrossed refuge of rafters for the doves to get out of the blistering winter winds and the cold. Some nights I'd dream long lines of them perched motionless, a tiny halo of light illuminated behind each feathery, bent head.

"C'mon. Enough already," my mom said. "Enough for one night." But my dad turned and limped into the kitchen instead, where he emptied an ice cube tray into a hand towel, which he folded and pressed against his left cheek and eye, the socket's black-and-blue orbit spiraling inward, and the crooked elastic waistband of his floral print skirt riding low on his hips. On the dinner table, his portion of the pork chops congealed in their white fat, and a single corn muffin off to the side, and my dad silent and hungry for nothing but an honest paycheck for an honest day's work slicing muscles and tendons, and now, that gone, his appetite piqued only by revenge.

My mom uttered not another word. It was well after midnight and she looked terrible, pale and gaunt, and she simply shook her head at my dad's ridiculous spin about the healing power of fisticuffs to clear both the air and the head. Cathartic was the word he used, though I wondered how cathartic are kidney kicks that leave you for weeks with blood in your pee?

October and no snow yet and Halloween just one week away, and there we were—father and son—sitting together on the back porch stairs, our eyes fixed not on the full moon or the stars but on the way the light's gauzy blue illumination covered only that part of the yard where both the llamas were buried, dead to some disease that only my mom, whose pets they were, could possibly pronounce. She was smart that way and knew the Latin names for shrubs and trees and birds and, had she ever been asked, could have delivered mass in that ancient and mysterious tongue that even the catechism nuns always mangled for us with their mumbles and their bowed black-and-white heads.

"Smoke?" my dad asked, and after my standard no thanks he said, "That's my boy," and pulled a flattened pack of Pall Malls from under a white satin garter and lit up, and draped the skirt hem back over his bony knees, covering not runs but wide angry rips in the nylons.

I assumed they were my mom's, a woman who, as my dad maintained, deserved a better shake in this life, but what she got was him, and he hadn't been real easy on either of us lately, though come judgment day I'd testify before God that he was not a cruel or heartless man. On other, lesser counts, guilty as charged, and I felt gut-certain that this latest one would go badly for us, and so when my dad mentioned a police blotter, I imagined it soaking up all our blood.

"It's likely not a prison crime," he said. "Nobody died or lost an eye, but there was a mess made, and most of it by yours truly. So yeah, I'd place this under the general heading of pretty bad."

"Did you start it?" I asked, and he said, "Henry, you go into Ma Dieter's bar dressed like this, like some Chatty Cathy, and ask if it's happy hour yet and if any of the mothers present got change for a three-dollar bill, you gotta like your chances. Odds are you'll get exactly what it is you came for."

He was not a big man, wiry and square-shouldered, maybe five-foot-eight is all, but in that outfit those out-of-proportion Popeye forearms engorged from all that lifting and cleaving of beef and swine seemed downright lethal, like wielded sledgehammers dead-centering a cattle spike and driving it like lightning deep into the brainpan. Plus, he had a speed bag in the garage, which he'd sometimes tattoo in rhythmic, symbolic pummeling of serious but lesser betrayals—promotions turned down, vendettas played out—"But you take away a man's livelihood, you leave him without any income at all, he'll go into survival mode and there's no telling what madness might take hold. Maybe I crossed the line tonight," he said. "But someone calls you a slut or strumpet and that catches hold, you best remind that someone about the virtue of keeping his damn mouth shut."

"Why'd someone call you that?" I asked, trying but unable to ignore how he was dressed.

"Henry, listen to me, okay? It's like this. Sometimes on the line there's bad stuff transpires, stuff I can't abide. Violations. And if you don't buddy with those at fault to just let it pass—just let it go, Frank—they don't like that, and they let it be known. And suppose midmorning the metal doors to the killing area get padlocked. And the FSIS inspectors are there with their cameras and clipboards, and failing grades mean fines are handed down—steep fines—and who's everybody looking crosswise at? Later someone sidles up to you and says, 'Whores galore,' and not in a good-natured sort of way. Trust me, the next Biblical flood arrives, they'll be the ones throwing the animals off the Ark."

I knew my mom wanted another pair of llamas, maybe by next spring if she was feeling better, though most of the talk I'd overheard had more to do with paying down debts. Like the three hundred bucks my dad owed some lug named Norman Martel who spent way too much time at the bleed rail, cracking jokes with his bullhorn voice. And stitched in block tomato-red letters across the wide back of his supervisor's coat: MEAT YOUR MAKER.

Not to mention the pickup's clutch slipping so badly that my dad had to take the long route home from work so as not to get caught downshifting between midnight and dawn—depending on his hours—just to make that slight rise in the distance beyond those endless fields of standing corn. Lying awake some nights I'd remember the pickup's window rolled down, me riding shotgun, and the radio cranked and my dad belting out, "And he's bad, bad Leroy Brown / The baddest man in the whole damn town," his all-time favorite tune, which these days when it came on only made him go silent.

I hoped he didn't have any plans to settle this latest dispute with anything but his two fists. That was bad enough, given how bad could run pretty deep with the local economy already up to its elbows in what my dad deemed the proverbial slop. Prosperity in these parts meant hitting the lotto, and he'd spent plenty trying, playing, week after week, variations on that same unlucky combination of our three birthdays. My mom had forgotten to take in the laundry, and my dad pointed out at all of his ankle-length white aprons hanging on the line, one for each working day. I didn't say so, but they looked like ghost torsos, bleached and slightly billowy from the breeze, and nothing but darkness underfoot.

He gestured as if to say, never mind that, and snubbed out his cigarette, and peeled off the remaining two or three press-on nails, which he flicked out into the grass. Then he slowly rubbed his fingertips with his thumbs, his left one sewn back on two different times, and my dad in a cast back on the job the very next day, an injury waiver already signed. Not back on the slaughter line, but rather checking levels in the hog waste cesspools where the flies amassed and buzzed all summer, or hosing watery cow turds into the concrete gutter troughs.

I figured some measure of sleep was already taking place in his mind, given how quiet he'd gotten, and I calculated that if I got up to go to bed he'd simply follow my lead and tomorrow we'd all wake a step or two closer to our imminent selves, my mom's upbeat turn of phrase in a crisis. Which of course she hadn't said lately, and I'd grown well enough acquainted over the years with how trouble had a way of following certain people around, and how reading trouble in our house did not mean reading between the lines.

Still, the way he looked seemed like punishment and humiliation enough, and possibly might have been, but when I got up and he said, "Henry, this isn't over and whatever gets said, whatever that might be . . ." it put to rest any hope that we'd slide by this night quite so easily.

Above us my mom's knuckles *rap-rapped* the windowpane, and my dad, already leaning back on his elbows, bent his head even farther back to stare up at her, though I noticed as I knelt down in front of him that only a few blurry stars were reflected there. The Corona Borealis, I thought. And not another single sound from anywhere as I unlaced his shiny black knee-high hooker boots and leveraged them off, one at a time, my hands and arms straining to free both of his cramped and blistered heels. No way did those boots belong to my mom, not in this or in any previous life or fantasy that I could imagine, and I hadn't a clue where he'd dug them up.

"Ah, that's much better," he said. "That's good, Henry. Now help your old man up, would you?" I could almost feel the tremor in his thighs as he stood and steadied himself for a moment on my shoulder and, still grimacing, he said to me, "Doing the right thing is hard enough. And to do that thing right is a whole lot harder, and all a person can do is work up the nerve to try. At least there's that," he said, "and precious little else that holds up for long in a person's life. To believe otherwise is just another mealy-mouthed, chicken-shit lie."

Oh, right, my mom would have said, paving the road to the poorhouse with all the best intentions. But I nodded nonetheless, as if his words supported my view exactly of what a father *should* stand for in the face of any injustice. In all fairness, his sermon wasn't that much different from what the nuns preached about our actions reflecting our hearts. And not to worry, as my mom so often reassured me, saying, "He just comes apart. But never all the way apart," though I wondered this time if he had, and if she was still up there watching us negotiate the stairs in the moonlight.

"Goodnight," my dad said once we were inside, the door closed and locked behind us, and my mom's black choir robe pressed and laid out on the recliner. Nobody had mentioned *not* attending mass in the morning at Saint Francis, the patron of kindness to animals, for whom my dad was named. Saint Frank. He who had worked twenty years in the same slaughterhouse and ate his meat rare and without apology, and hated the way that lone wolf paced and paced all day in his cage at the zoo. He who had sat next to me in the same up-front pew every week, where we prayed while my mom poured out over the entire congregation a music so pure that I believed her voice, and hers alone, would forever and ever save us in our time of need.

The storm did arrive, and deep in some strange dream space the wind chimes outside sounded like cow bells, like a slow herd of them crossing the creek, not toward the barn but straight into the chutes of the slaughterhouse, where the mushroom-stunner failed to knock down an enormous, gorgeous white bull. His eyes burned red, the high arc of his pee so golden it sparked each time he leapt and roared, as if to signal those cows to stop and turn around before the drop gate descended.

Then they passed right by me, all alone on the line, though I could hear my mom crying from somewhere far off, and Roger Cluff, the notorious ninth-grade sex fiend and bully, suddenly older and uglier, appeared by the scalding vats, where he exceeded yet another ear-piercing octave each time he squealed, "It's not the length, it's not the size—it's how many times you can make it rise."

The cows, leg-shackled and hanging upside down, limp and milky-eyed, barely even twitched when the sticker slit their jugulars. My fingers steamed as I tried to stem the hemorrhaging while the throats of the floor drains gurgled with blood. Or was it human laughter boiling up as that white bull's endless torment echoed out into the pastures each time someone cranked up the voltage, cranked it so high that brass ring through his nose turned molten.

Where was my dad? Where was Sister Regina? There was a terrible story here, and a problem with God, who appeared as no more than a headwind slowing by so many seconds the arrival of two transport trailers hauling beef cattle from opposite coasts, one from Oregon, the other from a farm in upstate New York. I crossed myself, and right there where the imaginary lines intersected, and because there were no traffic lights or stop signs or cautions of any kind, it was ordained that those thundering, slat-sided semis would arrive simultaneously, each traveling at precisely seventy-five miles per hour into the blue heart of the heartlands just before dawn.

On impact, the sky turned a muted pink, and I awakened sweating and startled by the smell of sausage sizzling, and my mom calling my name from downstairs, and I felt both saved and blessed as I hurried down to breakfast. The scrambled eggs the way I liked them, not too dry, were just sliding out of the skillet onto my plate, which my mom handed to me as I sat down next to my dad in his normal place at the head of the table. I knew just how hard to spin the lazy Susan so the grape jam would rotate exactly twice around before stopping directly in front of me, followed by a reverse half spin for the butter dish.

I'd never before seen my dad sip orange juice through a straw, or shake his head no when my mom offered a warm-up on his coffee, or order us in no uncertain terms not to answer the phone, though all three of us listened intently to the voice on the machine: "First find your pig, Frankie," and the sound of someone else snorting and grunting in the background, and the receiver eased back into its cradle.

"Probably just a wrong number," I said, and my dad said back, "Not hardly," making clear as he stared first at my mom and then at me that we'd be screening all calls for the time being. Which I hoped wasn't really necessary, but it took maybe four minutes for the ringing to begin again.

"We'll be there for the burning," a coarser, nasal voice said, at which point my dad put down his coffee mug and picked up and, instead of the outburst I figured would commence, said, "It's Sunday morning. The only thing burning here is the fog," which must have been what my mom was looking at out there in the field, her back toward us, and first light coming in through the window. The varicose veins low down on her legs had gotten worse, branching out blue above her calves, and the way she hugged herself so tightly made the whole kitchen go suddenly cold.

I could only hear my dad's half of the conversation, of course, which was brief, and he said, "Then take it on faith," and hung up, and unplugged the phone from the wall jack.

Her back still to us, my mom said, "So this is how we're going to live? Skip mass and hide out here in our own little corner of the world until you heal back up? And what then, Frank?" she said. "What's our strategy after that?" And when she turned around to face him, the emptiness in her eyes frightened me way more than any possible number of anonymous phone threats.

There was no playacting this time for my sake, though my dad might have responded better, or better yet, said nothing at all. My mom, turning his statement into a question verbatim, said, "The price of admission? That's it, Frank? That's your answer? Well, terrific, because we sure have paid for it, haven't we? The absolute best seats in the theater."

When he didn't answer, she said something about the boonies and living among men who slap their girlfriends into marrying young, as if the brute force of love were merely a kindness, a show of affection gone too far. I did not at my age care to examine the implications in that, though even then I felt the impossible shifting weight of things both valued and abused, and therefore lost. So I was glad when my dad got up abruptly and turned on the radio on his way outside. Turned it up too loud, but just in time for me to hear Paul Harvey signing off, as he always did in that strange, hesitating way he had of saying, "And now . . . you know the rest . . . of the story. Good day." I hoped against all odds that maybe it could be. So I gulped and swallowed and followed my dad, who was already inside the cab of the pickup, revving the cold engine, and the passenger door opened for me.

The muffler was doing its job, but when my dad let out the clutch so little gravel erupted that any visible evidence of an angry departure did not exist. I could tell by the way he gripped the steering wheel that he'd wanted badly to power the Dodge into fishtailing down the driveway to the blacktop road, and maybe leave some rubber where he hung a slow right instead toward town.

We said nothing for a while, and it didn't at that point seem clear to me that he did or did not have a specific destination in mind, and was maybe following nothing more than an urge to be gone from the mounting tension inside our house.

Not all the leaves were down yet, but last night's rain and wind had thinned them pretty good, and I liked the way they sounded slapping up wet under the snow tires that my dad always kept on year-round and rotated after each plowing season, so at least the pickup didn't shimmy. But sometimes the whole road seemed to if the Cedar River rose high enough outside its banks, the landscape swirling back and forth like the whole world was out of balance. I'd seen it happen a few times. But only once did my dad ever stop on Brown Bridge and take out from behind the seat his .22 pump with the long tube magazine, and let me shoot tiny eyes into those pumpkins that had floated up and away from the low-lying fields and into the river's main current. I hoped the rifle was not with us on this run, though I sure didn't intend to cross-examine him about that or, for that matter, anything else.

He lit a cigarette and lowered his visor, and when he cracked his window I could feel the wintry air rush in and the heavy swirl of his Aqua Velva drift across my neck and cheeks. He had appeared at breakfast clean-shaven, his thick hair combed back, but the half shadow on his face made his shiner seem even blacker.

The sky had turned from pink to orange, and up ahead two deer bounded across the road—way up ahead—so when my dad braked hard it was not to avoid them but rather to execute a dangerous U-turn, the passenger-side tires sliding off the wet pavement and bottoming, and then grabbing just enough of the shoulder to keep us from flipping over into the drainage ditch. In the space of maybe a couple of blinks he'd changed or made up his mind about something, and by the time we passed our house, the green speedometer needle had just nosed past seventy-five, but fell back to less than half that as we finally crested Wayne Hill. I wondered if my mom had seen or heard us speed by in the opposite direction from which we'd started out not fifteen minutes earlier. And if she had, whether she was every bit as frightened and confused and as knotted up in the stomach as I was.

I'd never once been in the slaughterhouse, though other kids whose dads worked there had, so I'd heard the grizzly accounts of giant blood clots breaking loose and spraying a fine red mist that hung for long seconds in the frigid air. Severed legs, the scooped-out skull-cradles of cows—details that always made me a little woozy and that I never, ever checked out with my dad, silently hating whatever part of him might have contributed to making those impossible-to-listen-to stories true.

It defied all logic, given how he loved my mom's llamas, and stayed up day and night with them in their slow dying, petting their necks and ears, talking softly and pressing cold washcloths to their lips and gums. My mom said he would have made such a gentle, compassionate veterinarian, but college for him never had much bite, and from way back our lives turning out a better way had proven to be an irregular thing.

His livelihood was what it was, or had been until those growing hostilities spilled over, eventually rendering him both vulnerable and defenseless but also, and unlike my mom, bitter and unafraid. It was no secret that he'd taken a position against the sadistic treatment of cows and hogs and goats. Which in turn, and over time, had brought the two of us—on a given Sunday morning in late October 1985—to be sitting in his red pickup with the engine off, and him asking me if I wanted to go inside.

"Your call," he said. "Because I have some tools to pick up," meaning his meat cleavers and boning knives, I guessed, and I flinched when he reached over and touched my shoulder. "You stay here then," he said. "Anybody comes by, you tell them I'll be right out." And he held up his key to show me he wasn't breaking in. "Right?"

"Right," I said, though he'd parked well off the road behind some sumac thickets, and a good distance from the slaughterhouse parking lot for a reason, and that reason seemed obvious to me.

"Okay. Good," he said. "I'm almost done here, and once I get back and this is all behind us, we'll come up with a workable plan. Whatever that might be. But for now the only thing you need to think about, the only thing you *must* remember, Henry, is that you and me—we were never here."

"Never," I repeated, a lie I wanted badly to believe but knew even then was no more than a weak-minded plea to insinuate ourselves away from the trouble ahead. And yet I could not think of a single other word to say.

He nodded then and checked his watch and started walking down a steep pitch of green field that leveled off after a ways, where he stopped and separated two strands of barbed wire before ducking through and waving back up at me.

He'd left the truck key in the ignition and I wondered if I could tune in that radio station from Winnipeg I'd found one night while the two of us were out just cruising the countryside like we used to do.

For sure there were places around with higher elevations, but I could still see over the slaughterhouse roof and beyond the feedlots and box-cars all the way to Lake Tonawanda, and figured maybe with the day so clear the radio reception would carry right out of the country. But what I heard before I ever even touched the on/off dial were the distant cries of snow geese, a huge raft of them lifting away from the lake's opal-colored surface. I'd say two hundred at least, their wings rippling in slow motion like light blue ribbons as they ascended above the tree line.

I got out and climbed into the bed of the pickup just to get a few feet closer to them, and my dad stopped and looked up right as they passed overhead. A non-hunter his whole life, he did not take aim down the length of his arms. He simply pointed skyward and then continued on, getting smaller and smaller until all I could see of him was that strange other image I tried *not* to conjure up inside my head. But the truth was simple: my dad in strumpet attire had cut a pretty unforgettable figure. And, because news always travels with fury in a small town, I knew that tomorrow at school I'd have to face the terrible reality of defending what he'd done, and possibly a whole lot more.

The snow geese kept rising, almost out of sight, and I thought then about how distance equaled velocity times time, how long before they'd put down again, and how often they'd be fired at and just how many would die on their long migration home.

My dad had bought the pickup used and had never removed the rear-window decal of the Grand Canyon, and talked back then about road trips he had in mind for us, oceans we ought to see, though I had yet to cross state lines in any direction, and I was glad not to hear it spoken of as an option on that particular day. Not that I much wanted to be where we were, either, and the agreement that we hadn't been here meant lies and alibis, what Sister Regina called the very longest route to paradise.

I folded my hands and placed them on top of the cab and rested my chin in the fleshy circle of forefingers and thumbs, and waited there for the slow weight of the sun to warm me. I can't say how long, or what transpired during my dad's absence, but when I saw him again he was running toward me, the long back of a stark white butcher's coat flapping out behind him. No knife or meat cleaver blades glittered in his fists, but he was holding something, a book or a ledger. When he raised it above his head, I thought maybe he was signaling to me to start the pickup for a quick getaway, and the blood chugged hot in my ears until I realized there was nobody in pursuit, nobody anywhere around. Just me, an accomplice who had dozed off momentarily, and my dad approaching fast and out of breath and saying as he arrived, "Easy as you please. Now come on, Henry, get down and let's get the holy hell gone from here."

We slow-poked our way home without much talk, the clutch so bad that my dad shifted without it, and without grinding the upper gears too badly. My mom had started a fire in the wood stove, smoke pouring out of the chimney as we pulled up. I could see her rinsing plates at the sink and stacking them in the dishwasher. Which on Sunday mornings ever since she'd gotten sick was my job, and I wished then that we'd come back with cider and some squash and warty gourds and maybe a few pumpkins to carve, the cold smell of fall all over us as we entered the kitchen. But only I went inside, empty-handed and saying, "Hi, Mom," and then running right upstairs to my bedroom, where I stretched the blinds tight to the windowsills and slid fully dressed between the sheets and pulled the quilt right up to under my eyes.

My mom had talked from time to time about selling and moving closer to town, but as a family we'd never lived anywhere else. Two stories plus the cellar and attic, and some old ornament work along the cornices. Four acres is all and, as I said, a barn that had fallen in, but the house was big and sturdy in the wind, which I liked, though there were certain spots in the hallway that even my mom's soft-soled moccasins made squeak.

I heard her approaching and then stop right outside my door. She didn't knock or talk or move. She just stood there in the heavy silence of whatever she was thinking until my dad whistled his way into the kitchen with an armload of logs that he dropped with a loud crash into the wood box. And then he called her name. "Annie?" And then a second time, not full boil, but louder, and that's when I pulled the pillow over my head and pressed my thumb knuckles so hard to my ears that nothing, for as long as I could stand it, could ever filter through.

I did not brighten up in Sister Regina's class, for sure not when it came to solving story problems. Nor did I resort to tears or rage as Roger Cluff's acne flamed with each foul-mouthed taunt he hurled just inches from my face. All fall he smelled like a smokehouse, and I knew he helped his dad, who, after the slaughterhouse was temporarily shut down, processed wild game in his garage.

"Spineless," Roger Cluff called me, and bent over and pressed his snout close to my ear and grunted like a warthog. "You cost us bigtime, you pussy twit," he'd whisper. "Goddamn traitor, you and your faggot old man." His eyes would blur and I could feel with each word the hate expanding all the way from the very back of his skull.

His hands at fourteen were already muscled, his cut thumbs cocked first thing each morning and the barrel-tips of his index fingers aimed right at my temples. Always full-faced. Always right up close and saying, "Ka-boom, Ka-boom. You're dead, faggot ass. You're dead fucking meat."

Although my mom asked for names, I refused to squeal on anyone, my clenched fists screaming silently from deep in my pants pockets. Except when I'd get home and go into the garage and swing wildly at the speed bag, connecting solidly only when it hung still, the round red leather stained with the sweat of my dad's knuckles. Sometimes just hanging there, it reminded me of some giant animal's heart. I'd promised my mom no schoolyard fights, had sworn to it on the Bible, no matter the volume of blows I absorbed during each school day's verbal melee.

I even lost a stare down to Marilyn Vanderbeam, a girl who sat across from me and whose gray eyes rivaled the favorite marbles in my collection, those with the smoky swirls inside. I'd taken to thinking for a while that I could love someone like her later on in life. Someone who wrote poems on black paper with white ink, poems about angels and God and one she read aloud about the risen soul of her border collie. But after my dad's trouble, she'd raise her chin in contempt and bead in on me in a way that made even my knees and elbows ache.

In December Sister Regina decorated the classroom with angels and doves, the manger alive with painted plaster wise men and camels, and a single donkey who seemed so peaceful curled up by himself in the straw. Seated at our desks we'd sing "O Holy Night" and "Joy to the World."

Sister Regina fingered her rosary and lectured us on what she referred to as "this season of mercy." But she rarely called on me anymore, not even to wipe down the blackboard or go outside into the snow to whack the erasers free of chalk dust, all that knowledge dissolved into so many tiny cloudbursts. I could see the angry blue veins pulse low on her forehead whenever I raised my hand, a habit I finally broke that same week my dad started serving his sentence for damages inflicted on Ma Dieter's bar and on a certain clientele of slaughterhouse regulars, a fine he outright refused to pay. Not back then would he pay, and as he made clear to my mom, "Not ever. Not one stinking dime," though it cost him ninety days at Camp Pugsley, a low-security penal facility less than an hour's drive north toward the Straits.

Against my mom's advice he waived his right to a court-appointed attorney, arguing that the case against him was nothing more than spite and revenge. "Ma Dieter's," he said. "Good Christ. What's Ma Dieter's got to do with any single goddamn thing?"

It was late and they were alone in the kitchen and I'd sneaked into listening range just in time to hear him confess what everyone suspected and said but could not prove. That he was the whistleblower. Not a mole, but just some local nobody who'd refused to serve what he did not believe in and could not cure. "Your dad's *non serviam*," as my mom would later refer to it, but never without that sharp edge for the terrible, terrible price we all paid.

He'd struck no deal with anyone, but it was agreed nonetheless that his name, Francis Henry Burke, would, for his and for his family's protection, nowhere be mentioned. Nor would he ever—profiled by his fellow workers as a crazy, disgruntled employee currently serving time for assault—be called to testify as an eyewitness against the evils of human cruelty. They did not need him to appear in court, the case against the slaughterhouse airtight.

Before he left he had a new clutch installed in the pickup. And both times I talked with him on the phone, he joked about making potholders and key chains, and how maybe he'd market them once he got released. It was hard to imagine him spending too much time doing arts and crafts. I figured they'd have him deboning chickens or trimming fat off the low-end steaks and chops, but maybe knives in the hands of criminals violated some fundamental code of law.

We had an unlisted phone number by then, and my mom spent part of every day talking with the real estate fellow who'd listed our house and who, given the circumstances, convinced her to reduce the price.

It sold shortly after that, sight unseen, to the manager of the new Arby's already under construction in Roscommon, a town with a future about ten miles away. My mom borrowed against the sale and in that way arranged for a moving van, had a new muffler installed on the pickup, and padded her checkbook in order to keep pace with the torrent of ordinary bills.

My dad asked us not to visit, and we didn't, not once. But when he got released on his own recognizance for two days at Christmas, we drove up to Camp Pugsley to get him. My mom put on a dress I liked, something she'd found while cleaning out the closets. A dress from another era, I thought, that made her look younger and pretty again, and I saw her almost smile into the full-length mirror as she turned in slow half circles, first left and then right before she closed the door.

"You look nice, Mom," I said, which maybe I shouldn't have, given that right then her neck muscles tightened and she closed her eyes. She held a purse in one hand and took out a Kleenex, at which point I left to go shovel a path to the pickup and to scrape ice from the wind-shield. My mom did not like driving any distance with the snowplow attached, so my dad had taken it off, and I noticed as soon as I got outside that somebody had come by in the dark and made a swipe of our driveway. I had no idea if my dad had hired it done or if in secret a Good Samaritan on his way to work just wanted to do a decent thing.

In the truck she talked about Ohio, where we'd be moving shortly after the holidays, and where I'd be enrolled in a new school. "Nobody will know us there," she said. "Henry, nobody."

Right then, a sunlit cloudburst of snow turned everything bright white, a Michigan squall, and we slowed to a crawl for maybe ten min-utes before the windswept world of scrub oaks and fields reappeared, first in patches, and then the whole road finally opened up again. I didn't ask, but I wondered if my dad would be wearing one of those orange jumpsuits with numbers on the back. And if my mom's purse would be searched by the guards, and if I'd be patted down before the two of us were led into some sterile visiting room as my dad was escorted through a maze of security doors, each one buzzing open as he approached.

There was none of that. Instead, he was waiting for us outside the main gate, dressed in his polar-fleece vest and jeans and shifting from foot to foot and working a cigarette hard. No hat or scarf or suitcase, though I could already from that distance see a red bow sticking out from each of his vest pockets. Presents he'd made or bought? We hadn't put up a tree or stockings or even a front door wreath, the liv-ing room piled high with taped and labeled boxes.

When he saw the pickup, he cocked his head and took a final, slow drag and then held out his thumb like a hitchhiker. He appeared thin, and, as he walked toward us, his boot heels kicked up tiny parachutes of feathery new snow, blanketing the sirens I expected at that instant to erupt.

My mom did not open the door or slide over next to me. Instead she rolled down the window and my dad leaned low and asked if we were going his way. The mustache he'd grown was mostly gray. And the way he locked onto my mom's eyes and gripped the door with both hands made me momentarily light-headed, as if the world's slow rotation had suddenly speeded up. My chest felt both empty and full, like I could breathe and couldn't at the same time.

It wasn't a real long kiss, but long enough for my dad to reach behind her so I could hold tight to his hand until the spinning stopped. Which it did, and suddenly all that had befallen us seemed, if not a blessing, then something approximate to that. Something, I thought, ready at that moment, to bear its weight and be graced.

[Long After the Sons Go Missing]

PLAYING OVER AND OVER in Karl Radoszkowicz's head is not his wife's insistent caution for him to wear his safety harness but his promise to her that he does—Always, without exception, he tells her, cinched tightly—when in fact he has never even owned one, not in all his years of bow hunting. And the cell phone he claims to carry with him right up into his tree is turned off almost half a mile out of reach on the front seat of his Ford Explorer. Not that it matters.

He has plummeted fifteen feet from his stand and has only a few minutes ago reawakened to an intermittent early November snow, the cold fat flakes melting on contact with his face. It is streaked black and green and brown. Otherwise he detects no bodily sensation anywhere, not the slightest pulse or tingling, his legs spread-eagle, his arms limp at his sides. For a few additional seconds he doesn't even recognize or remember where he is, as if he has just exited a strange and lingering dream and can't yet determine if he is hurt or bruised or marked in any way, if his bones or vertebrae are still intact.

Except for the faint murmuring of his heart, Karl Radoszkowicz wonders, without any physical pain or panic, if he is alive. *Yes*, he thinks. Yes I am, because when he attempts to say this he can move his lips, his tongue, and when he tries to speak his wife's name floats up in a thin breath-cloud and disappears: Irena, whispered so softly he can barely hear it, his throat gone tight with the effort.

Karl's quiver is still attached to the bow, the bow to the dangling rope, the arrows' incandescent orange-and-blue fletching turning soundlessly in a slow-motion circle above him. Like candle flames, he thinks, aglow in the dying light at the swamp edge where he sits every evening, all season long, whenever the wind conditions are right. It's the old ache of being invisible and alone that he craves, sealed off from the steady low-grade buzz and clatter of his life, though he has never actually articulated this, not really, other than to let the deer pass and pass more often now that he has turned sixty.

He is an even six feet tall and just overweight enough so that he can't quite see the toe-tips of his hunting boots beyond his stomach. But he can, by shifting his eyes, focus on how his fingerless gloves remain cupped, as though frozen stiff or perhaps still clutching onto that snapped oak branch that has always, in his confident outward lean, supported him in the past. Just this morning at breakfast, when Irena reminded him that he wasn't a kid anymore, he shrugged it off, a gesture of pretense that served only to remind him how agile he still feels—all flex and bend—each time he climbs or descends that natural ladder of limbs. She should see me, he thought, this graceful up-and-down dance he's preformed so many times in the pitch dark that he could do it blindfolded. The way he makes love to her some nights with his eyes squeezed shut, imagining not another woman but the sweep of his own wife's wavy auburn hair. And the airy bones of her back and the open wings of her shoulder blades hovering above him on the bed as he remembers her just ten years ago, before their marriage turned recalcitrant and remote and entered what Karl recognizes now to be survival mode.

Sometimes full days vanish with barely a spoken word between them. Entire conversations orchestrated with their eyes, like sign language they pretend not to understand, though there are those other moments, too, when one of them smiles or nods and everything solitary and distant begins to dispel into the simulated patterns of an enduring and happier past.

They talk. They sleep again in the same bed, carefully touching, less fearful of their affections; to the extent that Karl speculates about the solvency of their marriage, he's almost certain at such junctures that he can save it.

The more he believes this, the more he relaxes on that same thirty-minute drive outside the town limits. Past corn-stubble fields and that long-abandoned landfill stretch straight west to County Line Road, where he turns off the loose gravel and left onto a rutted, overgrown two-track and then left again before quick-swinging in four-wheel partway down the narrow logging cut and out of sight. And there, staring into the rearview mirror, he streaks his cheeks and nose with camo grease, then hides his car keys on the left front tire and, out of habit, checks his watch. Every detail timed so that he'll be settled in his stand before that first deer splashes across Hall Creek on its slow forage toward him. Karl hasn't yet this season drawn back, but he has daydreamed that trophy ten-point he's seen three times already into perfect, broadside kill-shot range.

By design no one has a clue as to Karl's whereabouts, and he has never—not once in the sudden popularity of this ancient and solemn rite—seen another hunter happen by. Nor has he ever encountered a game warden waiting for him out by the road, wanting to check his license. So the odds of quick rescue, Karl knows, now that he has regained full consciousness, appear far-fetched, the temperature dropping fast, and his camouflaged clothes too lightweight for the night ahead, his jacket still partly unzipped.

He wonders if he has started to shiver or if his lips are turning blue, his naked fingertips inviting frostbite. And why, when he closes his eyes against the snow, does he conjure up the image of his only son, Sam, who lives in California, the person, Karl believes, least likely in the entire world to walk out at dusk into this northern Michigan outback in search of him.

The two haven't spoken in nearly a decade. Not since Sam arrived home that Christmas with his partner, a clean-cut, early-30s loan officer or mortgage banker or something like that named Gil, a USC graduate, and the notion of them spending the weekend shacked up in the same bedroom had proved impossible for Karl to abide. Somehow the teak-framed waterbed he'd always hated made it seem even worse, that sudden imagined undulation of waves awash in his mind. There was, after all, the fold-out sofa in the den, which had in the past served as an overflow guest room when his folks were both alive but hard-pressed to negotiate the staircase to the second floor—his mom's cataracts, his dad's diabetic legs. Had Karl been home at the time he would have assumed the obvious, as he would have even if Sam's would-be had been female, and ushered whoever it was in that direction, into separate sleeping quarters.

He never could decide for certain whether or not Irena had known ahead of Sam's arrival that he'd be accompanied by this other and, as far as Karl knew, uninvited, never-before-mentioned stranger. Had Irena, in collusion with their son, sneaked behind Karl's back, consenting to such an arrangement and then remaining mute, leaving whatever transpired to chance? Had she, in essence, made and measured and left him to fend for himself, the odd man out? She who'd greeted these two young men at the Grand Rapids airport and driven them the two and a half hours back to the house while Karl, at work, calculated the benefits and risks of a counter-offer on that single-story warehouse over on Canal Street?

There was no question about the necessity for additional space. Old World Window & Door, which he'd founded, had prospered and grown, making him if not a wealthy man then a respected and mainstay member of the small business community in this small but slowly expanding throwback town. He was proud of the service plaques that hung in a straight line on the wall behind his desk and of the company's reputation for never once having been litigated or, as far as he knew, anywhere maligned, not even by his competitors. Karl Radoszkowicz, owner and company president, employer of seven full-time installers, has from day one stood behind his products with a certified lifetime warranty and a handshake. The same way he had always, as he once believed, stood firmly in the image of himself as a loving husband and father: honest, even-tempered, undefined by haste or recklessness or intolerance. It wasn't a posture. Karl was what he appeared, a square shooter whose easy demeanor and straight-ahead talk put others immediately at ease, and so whenever he spoke people listened.

But it was Sam doing most of the talking, about his medium: not job or occupation but "medium" in fabric design. "Leisure fashion," as he said, his collarless white silk shirt accented with silver buttons the size of quarters, and the billowy sleeves flared out like a carnival knife-thrower's, his bleach job highlighted some shade between orangeade and khaki. He seemed thinner, too, narrower-faced, the forced inflections of his voice awkwardly arranged. Like he was in a play, Karl thought, the gay and witty lighthearted lead in this contemporary family holiday comedy where everyone long absent and therefore changed gets reacquainted and closer than ever. And wasn't that the correct message for the season? Rejoice, rejoice? Karl thought no, possibly not, the Christmas tree up and decorated and the fiber-optic angel on top turning brilliant pewter. Then platinum. Then blue bleeding into lavender, into magenta, the different hues like vapors spreading out and dissolving in every direction across the fleck-textured ceiling. A dozen or more presents were wrapped and stacked underneath, shiny gold lamé stick-on bows and an oversized wreath with spray-painted white pinecones accenting the front door, artificial icicles hanging from the eves.

At no point had Karl been clued in on his son's scheduled departure, and although he didn't inquire he secretly hoped it would be sooner than later and, insofar as their stay might possibly be open-ended, he thought, No way. Not on his watch it wouldn't, not under the existing circumstances, and given how he'd arrived home to find his house guests not so much comfortably settled in as having taken the place over. Gil, clad in black, vintage Johnny Cash, had, in advance of the dinner hour, showered and shaved and poured himself a Jameson's on the rocks from the cut-glass decanter, and was relaxing, legs up and crossed at the ankles, in Karl's recliner, from which position he shook his host's outstretched hand and canted back, smiling and, Karl sensed, sizing him up. The new professionals, and who'd believe it: just a single generation removed. Was it the malfunction of the cerebrum or the cortex or was it some cultural disinclination that made a person want to fancy up and react with such stern disregard for everything that preceded them?

Karl had never known anyone named Gil before, as in girl without the *r*, a consideration he kept to himself but later wondered if Gil had been the one who'd cranked the thermostat up like that. Eighty degrees at least when Karl had first stepped inside out of the cold, his brain made suddenly noisy and hot by the odd and pervasive festivity filling the house, that buzzy open laughter and Bing Crosby's "White Christmas" assailing him through the stereo speakers. And turn that down, Karl then said to himself, uncharacteristically assertive; Grinch-like and without explanation or apology, he requested that the heat be left where he had set it and the audio volume as well, simple, fundamental domestic matters these young men from Sausalito would either warm to or not.

As a joke they put on matching sweatshirts with the hoods up, drawstrings pulled tight, and sat down side by side at the dining-room table, the candle flames adrift in that middle distance between Karl and his guests each time they shivered and blew into their close-cupped palms. And Irena all swoons and giggles as if the mere sight of them clowning around and cajoling like that defined, to its full extent, a deeply profound delight long absent from her life.

The antics abated not one iota, each new ad lib stagier than the last, which might in part explain why, midway through the meal, Karl tapped his wine glass with the outside of his wedding ring and announced in the resounding quiet, "I think it best that the two of you pack up and be on your way. Right now," he said. Just like that, from one to the other, his voice oddly calm after the taut and silent gritting of his teeth while he'd feigned, all evening, polite if distant accord.

It was of course the most reckless, wrongheaded thing he could have said, which Karl reflexively understood even before Irena touched his elbow and implored him not to overreact. "Don't," she said, her face flushed red. "Please. You're blowing this all out of proportion. They're only having fun. They're mocking themselves, for gracious sakes; can't you see that?" And to Sam, "Your father, he's . . . he doesn't mean it the way you think."

But he did mean it, every carefully enunciated syllable, and in that same enflamed but quiet rage he pressed the issue by pushing himself slowly up from the table, his pulse thrumming in his neck as he stood and leaned as far forward as he could, fixing first on Sam and then on Gil with a stare that startled and frightened even him.

Neither uttered another word, their eyes averted, and Karl himself—as he has since and often—might have conceded right then that both of them had in turn politely passed on the backstraps he'd marinated overnight and grilled on the flagstone patio, the sudden updrafts of wind heaving so hard that the whole house creaked and moaned around him. From outside, not ten feet removed through the glass slider, he had watched the three of them raise one showy, boisterous toast after another, laughing and leaning in so close together each time they clinked glasses that their foreheads touched.

Okay, Karl had thought, hugging himself against the gusts and the cold. And then, as he reentered the dining room, Fine. But why hadn't they said in advance they were vegans? Wasn't that the correct term—vegans? Leaf and seed eaters, scone-heads, as he'd heard his workmen wisecrack about the town's first macrobiotic restaurant, and he found it not only discourteous but also cowardly that Sam and Gil had concealed their aversion to red meat until the very instant Karl had begun to serve it, rare and seared perfectly in its juices. A feast, an offering as he saw it, and Judas Priest, wasn't some forewarning all he would have needed to stay if not neutral then at least tolerant enough not to have unloaded on them full-bore the way he did?

"It's the wine speaking," Irena had said in his defense, but it wasn't any such thing. In or out of the moment, Karl would have considered alcohol the flimsiest, most cowardly excuse of all. He had never in his life stumbled tipsy into provoking an argument or altercation, and he wasn't about to duck and ditch to ameliorate the situation with trumped-up pretenses, not even to win back the already reluctant trust of his one and only son.

No, it wasn't the wine. It was bow season then, too, the brutally frigid and demanding after-firearms stretch that had just reopened, and the fresh, fat-marbled venison ribs in the fridge had somehow entered the conversation. *Gross*, that bold and nakedly stated remark that Karl has never forgotten, though he can't swear who said it, Sam or Gil, as if they'd coupled as a single marauding voice set loose to berate everything that Karl's life had become, everything Neanderthal and midwestern.

And that, more than anything else, was what set him reeling, that queasy, overwilled, single-word assessment of this pursuit he loved and respected and that every succeeding year had less and less to do with killing. Yet it was the killing he described, calculated to disturb, something else he'd never before done or imagined doing. But there it was, entirely Jekyll-Hyde, and Karl didn't dial it down, detailing instead the circular incision around the anus, and the gutting-out of the animal, and how his arm had disappeared elbow-deep into the slick blue-veined chest cavity, the steaming arterial blood glowing crimson in the snow.

Gil, hands suntanned and folded on the table edge, had slow-nodded all doe-eyed when Sam pantomimed a gag. To Karl, the identical slantwise angle of their smirks constituted the crudest, most insensitive gesture of all. "Well then," Irena had intervened. "Maybe this might be a good time to change the subject." And it was shortly after that strained lull, during which nobody spoke or joked or caught anybody else's eye, that Karl had said and done what he did. It was, after all, his house, his right, and, that settled, need he say anything more?

Within the hour Irena was back from the Super 8 motel where she'd left Sam and his partner, a MasterCard charge that Karl refused the following month to pay or to acknowledge even to his own wife that anyone he knew and cared about had ever visited them from as far away as the dream coast only to end up staying the night in a cut-rate establishment like that.

When Karl opens his eyes it has stopped snowing. Although he can't see them in the dark cavernous amphitheater of the sky, he can hear the faint fugue-like barking of Canada geese far overhead, and those first few pinpricks of stars appearing not just distant but numb, like something viewed through water or frost. He assumes he is still breathing, although he can't feel the shallow rise and decline of his chest, his body weightless as if he might any second dissolve into millions of invisible particles and vanish forever into the thin, winter-pure air.

He can taste its coldness, like pure oxygen, and it comes to him that this might not be such a terrible way to go. No slow freezing to death or writhing through mud and scrub all night toward his SUV; more like entering into a peaceful dream, where, lying back, he might simply watch as his soul vaulted upward and away. He is almost giddy with the thought. *Yes*, he tells himself, alone in the sudden moonlight, its dull sphere close to full—a hunter's moon—its feathery halo illuminating the snowy, bluish ground all around him.

And so Karl lets himself go, adrift in a far-distant quietness so big he almost doesn't hear his mom's disembodied voice. But there's no mistaking it: much louder now, and she's scaring the life out of Karl, who is jolted back awake, trying to clear his mind while turning on the bedside lamp. They're on the phone, and Karl keeps pleading with her to slow down. "Slow down," he says, while his mom backslides faster and faster into those same raspy, harsh gutturals of inconsolable human grief that he knows well. All he can glean is that his dad has had a massive stroke, and, as if in the immediate aftermath of some blinding flashpoint inside his own brain, Karl registers not individual words or moans anymore but only the violent white light of his mom's inarticulate terror.

There's so much pressure at the back of Karl's throat that when he tries to swallow he can't, and nearly gags after hanging up and whispering in constricting gulps to Irena this horrible, unspeakable news. Sam, of course, is still at home. He's ten, a quiet, inward kid immured in sleep so deep that he hasn't even stirred, his bedroom door slightly ajar and his paternal grandfather dying just minutes before Karl—driving nonstop and crazed throughout the night into the predawn to be there by his hospital bedside—arrives.

What was it Karl needed to say to him? And what would he say right now, in this stricken condition, to Sam, who might this instant be on the phone with Irena. She calls him only when Karl is at work or out in the woods, not so much in conscious deception as in the essential privacy of his absence. They talk often. Karl knows this, and sometimes while up in his stand he'll imagine eavesdropping, whereas all he really ever hears is the silent, hypnotic drone and murmur of his own convoluted thinking, the line gone dead again and Karl whispering, *Hello?* Karl whispering, *Please, anything at all.* But what stands—what has always stood—is Sam's repeated refusal to speak to his father ever again, as if every door and window that Karl has ever sold has been slammed and nailed permanently shut.

Although he has never openly admitted it, Karl so badly wanted a son that he believed he had, by some act of divination, willed him to be a boy and secretly sought out far back in his mind, months before Sam was born, how they'd pal around, just the two of them, an unbreakable father-son allegiance in which every daydreamed escapade unfolded in perfect sync.

Factored big-time was that when Sam turned fourteen they'd bowhunt together, devising plans and strategies as Karl had done with his dad, scouting preseason for runways and sign and lopping off branches to create open shooting lanes, shadowed tunnel shafts where their broadheads would spiral down at light speed.

He remembers best helping skin and stretch and tan the hides, and the sound the knife blade made feathered across the whetstone, slowly back and forth until the steel edge could—as his dad used to say—trim the sidewalls right off a Fleetwood. "A Cadillac," he'd say to Karl, with leather seats and a vinyl top that he promised himself in retirement but never owned. He only ever drove used pickups, half- and three-quarter-ton Fords in constant need of repairs, which on the weekends he'd make himself, the ashtrays always stuffed with the stubbed-out butt ends of Pall Malls. Depression vehicles, as Karl's mom referred to them, with or without a capitol *D*, which his dad joked gave her something to both fret and dream about. "You betcha," he'd say, "a shiny new midnight-blue Fleetwood right off the showroom floor." Then he'd light another cigarette before leaning full weight above the hand drill, the 5/16-inch bit slow-boring a single hole through the partial skull plate. "There," he'd say, and blow the bone dust away and screw that newest set of antlers to the back wall of the garage. Some nights in the flood of the high beams, the door opening overhead, it looked like a whole herd of ghost bucks huddled up in there.

"Missed," Sam would say, his mantra no matter the amount of patient instruction Karl provided. Regardless of the number of practice tries, Sam remained incapable of hitting any part of the delta deer. A mere fifteen stationary yards away—a distance difficult to misjudge—and yet every shot zinging high or low or so far wide of the backstop hay bales that Karl speculated, even then, that his son might be missing on purpose. One evening, a massive purple-bruised cloudbank moving in, Karl's exasperation tempted him to point up and say to Sam—a dare, really—"There. See if you can hit that."

At twelve Karl could bull's-eye any target at twice that range, the cedar shafts grouped so tightly he'd grab a whole fistful at once, the circumference no bigger around than his skinny wrist. He loved that solid, flat *thawp* the field tips made—as he does still—and how hard they were to pull back out, his forearm muscles trembling.

"Just relax. The key is to get comfortable," he'd insist to Sam, "and do not blink or flinch. Firm grip, but there's no need to squeeze like you're trying to strangle it. The bow is merely an extension of your arm, okay? It's part of you. So draw back like I showed you, and remember, same anchor point every single time. That's better. That's it. Now concentrate not on the whole deer but on an imaginary spot right behind the front shoulder, and when your pin's dead-on, hold for another three-count, and then easy as you can into the shot. Go ahead. It'll happen, you'll see. You'll get it."

But he didn't get it, every release as jerky and uncoordinated as the last. And so it came to Karl as no real surprise when Sam, on that long-anticipated opening October morning, made apparent in no uncertain terms how stupid and pointless he believed this primitive hunting compulsion to be.

The exercise of rousting Sam at any hour was never a single-effort ordeal, and at five in the morning he had tunneled even farther under the blankets and pillows.

"C'mon, rise and shine," Karl had said, gently shaking him. "The Bigfoot Special's just about ready." Meaning blueberry pancakes and Canadian bacon and orange juice freshly squeezed. "Five minutes," he said, and when Sam didn't register in any way Karl hauled the heavy bedcovers back with a single swoop. "Hey, snap to, Natty Bumpo," he said. "Do you hear me? Let's move it. We gotta go."

Karl had laid out his son's new scent-proof hunting clothes and insulated waterproof boots the previous night, but when Sam finally padded into the kitchen he was barefoot and still wearing his pajamas, his eyelids half-mast as he squinted and blinked at the day's dark and premature arrival, as if to demonstrate his displeasure at trading away his dream time for this.

"What's the deal?" Karl said. "What's up?" Meaning, he knows now, what in the hell, his voice trailing off, holding back, yet the admonition of annoyance in his tone no doubt unmistakable. "Why aren't you dressed? Fifteen minutes max and we're out of here. Otherwise," he said, and shrugged, fingers splayed, palms up.

"I don't want to go," Sam said. "I don't want to hunt deer or anything else. Not this morning and not ever."

At first Karl only nodded as he turned away and moved the two simmering skillets to the off burners, the breakfast plates side by side on the counter. Then he turned back to Sam and said, "That true? You mean that?"

"Yes," Sam said, and Karl said back, "Since when?"

"Since always," Sam said. "Since forever." Which by Karl's calculations constituted pretty poor reaction time, an entire growing-up's worth to finally come to this, and he might have uttered something to that effect—a last-minute appeal for Sam to reconsider—had he not noticed him holding one of his homemade papier-mâché masks. He and Irena would spend endless hours making and painting them, like faces for a children's theater—dimpled and rosy-cheeked, nothing a boy who owned a compound bow and a drag rope would be caught dead wearing—and when Sam put it on Karl told him, "Stop. Take that off," its lips fat and lacquered pink, its eye slits so close-set and narrow that he could see only Sam's dark pupils dilating and staring out, leering, his wheat-colored bangs spilling over the high forehead.

Outside Karl could hear a car slow and then the folded-up newspaper skipping in its orange plastic sack across the driveway, much earlier than usual, and the car speeding up again and out of earshot. Somebody else, Karl guessed, in a hurry to get done and into the woods.

He wanted to tell Sam that two of his installers, an entire year in advance, had put in to get this day off. As Karl's dad always had, then working a double shift and keeping his son out of school if the opener fell on a weekday. A double bonus, and Karl so adrenaline-primed that he barely slept, up and dressed and downstairs before the alarm even sounded. He wanted to say that, too. I mean who knows for sure, right? One time, that's all I ask. A trial run, and then whatever you decide stands. Scout's honor. But far from removing the mask and sitting down to breakfast, Sam hung back, making no move other than to adjust the elasticized strap for a better fit. And then it hit Karl in a kind of spitfire flash that by whatever terms he might coerce his son into compliance, he would only, in the long run, make things even worse between them.

He trusted that Irena would get the gory details from Sam sometime after first light, listening without interruption as she shredded cheddar or provolone into their omelets. On the QT, Karl presumed, and never to be mentioned again, leastwise not to him. In her way, Irena had tried to prepare Karl, at first intoning subtle overtures half under her breath. Spare me, he'd think, and sometimes, without him ever asking, she would, but only to broach the subject again, and always more audibly. Advice he didn't want or need, his patience worn thin by her invented anxieties.

"All I'm suggesting is that you give him a wider berth," she'd say, "that's all," alluding to Sam's other interests and to his subdued or, as she put it, repressed inclinations to be himself around his dad. "Have you considered that he might not want to sit outside in the dark?" she'd say. "Have you, all alone high up on some perch?" as if she were describing a caged parrot or cockatoo. Utter nonsense, Karl insisted, plain and simple. She was dead wrong in a dozen different ways, and he took exception to her mantra that he of course "meant" well, but . . . inferring not that Karl was a bad father—she would never think that way—but rather that, like a lot of fathers who loved their sons, he'd been blinded by his own willed misperceptions. "Make room in your life for Sam to be himself, Karl," she'd say. "Do that for all of us, and before it's too late."

Maybe it had always been fated right from the get-go, although to Karl that seemed an easy and convenient exoneration. Not that he needed reasons to either condemn or condone but only to concede that something had, on a certain opening morning, come to its inevitable end. If so, he thought, if that's the final verdict, at least let it be said face-to-face, without any more disguises. Clean slate and move on.

But reaching out to remove the mask he felt suddenly light-headed, like vertigo, the whole room seeming to shift and tilt as if he'd placed the wrong end of his binoculars tight to his eyes, the reverse magnification making Sam appear tiny, a hazy, wavering outline so far distant that he all but disappeared. There and gone and never more than a literal arm's length away. It took only a few seconds for Karl to steady himself and blink the morning back into view: one one-thousand, two one-thousand, three one-thousand, the kitchen vacant and Sam nowhere in sight. Not a sign of him, as if he'd vanished into thicker cover, the way Karl, season after season, had seen those older, warier bucks do. Mere phantoms or figments, perhaps, and yet he could always feel them out there, invisible and watching him.

He didn't call after or follow Sam back upstairs. Instead he poured a cup of coffee for the road and put on his hunting hat and jacket and faltered outside, not in the direction of his car but into the backyard, where the window to Sam's bedroom was pitch dark. And Karl and Irena's bedroom, too. Dark enough, he believed, for a face to be pressed against the pane without him even knowing. And yet he imagined so clearly the slight inward curve of her thighs and her bare knees pressed to the floor that he pointed up, just in case, at the constellation of the deer, as if to say, Look. Right there, the patterns of our lives mirrored all around us. Karl's dad had taught him that. God's light and compass, he'd called it, for all the night prowlers disoriented or lost.

Karl is in and out of dreams. They overlap and mutate and he lets them come. In this one he steps so lightly that his feet don't make a sound, like he's floating through the house from room to room, completely unaware of his body. He can dim the lights simply by willing it, or steady the stepladder while Irena damp-wipes the ceiling fan's slightly canted blades into a softer glaze. He likes looking up at her singing to herself, something melancholy, something made up, her hemline waltz-length though it's been half a lifetime since they've danced cheek to cheek. But he can stop the clock now, the hard edge of every tick gone silent like the inside of that glass globe he used to hold up and shake. It's by far the best dream he has ever had.

But sad, too, and phantasmagoric, every domestic break and fracture fused, every painful curvature reversed and healed like uprooted trees tilting back upright into their original shapes. Falling slow-mo-

tion from one of them, Karl holds out his arms and upon impact another powdery snow angel explodes all around him. But this time he
can't get up. He can't even push himself into a sitting position. He's
that exhausted, a kid again, completely worn out and the world everywhere white-rimmed except for the moon's blue aurora, and his childhood house illuminated right there in front of him.

The picture window is as big as a movie screen, the light so brightly
projected that he almost closes his eyes. But there's his dad stoking the
woodstove and his mom pacing back and forth, hugging that same
brightly colored afghan shawl around her shoulders, the floor seeming to tremble beneath her footsteps. The temperature has continued
to fall, a few more bone-chilling degrees each night. It must be below
zero by now and this woman of a thousand hopes gone south, or whatever that phrase his dad sometimes uses to describe her winter moods.

A thousand hopes. At this moment Karl has one hope only: that
she'll stop and stare outside to where he's lying on his back, wishing
he could wave to her and that she would see him and wave back. Or
that he could somehow be standing right there in front of her, tap-tap-
ping on the glass. But there's no way to unlock his wrist or fingers or
raise his arm like his dad just did, lifting a bottle of beer to his lips—a
Pabst Blue Ribbon, which has never before made Karl thirsty but now
he is, like he's been eating salted peanuts all day. He's so thirsty he
can't even swallow, his tongue tip dry and pressed against the back of
his teeth, the chalky skin of his throat closing over. And there's a faint
but unmistakable odor of urine. He feels no warm dampness, but of
course there's no way he can check himself to be sure.

All he can summon are names, and they come to him easily—that
handful he loves and misses and mourns every day. Their faces waver
just beyond the spotlight that surrounds and, if he doesn't avert his
eyes, blinds him. Like somebody jacking deer, freezing them in their
tracks. But there are no shots fired, and through the noisy wind-chop
a voice like God's keeps calling down to him: *We're here. We've found
you. Stay awake, Karl, stay with us. We're taking you away,* as if they

mean to beam him up as soon as those who have gathered have said good-bye.

The first to lean in is his dad, two decades beyond his stroke and wearing that same suit and shoes he was buried in, older by far than any memory Karl has of him. Wizened and pallid, his face lopsided and tilted upward to where a man on a rope ladder lowers himself through the roaring turbo of light and wind, Karl's jacket billowing out and snapping.

And look, there's Karl's mom, propped up by a walker, smiling at him, but oh, sweet Jesus, her eyes—they're taped over with cotton and gauze. Karl prays she won't remove the bandages. Not here, not again, the whites so red veined and vascular the first time that he believed they were tiny twin hearts staring out at him. And then his dad, sobbing and gently kissing her lids. A miracle, he'd said, that she could see at all, everything occluded but with some luck and corrective lenses just maybe, over time, she would sit on the edge of Karl's bed and read to him. Like before, minus the magnifying glass and that cold compress pressed to her forehead, and always looking either left or right, nothing straight on ever quite in focus, nothing staying put. It's true, Karl thinks: The world really does move in half circles. First in one direction and then in the other, exactly like this, back and forth, snow blowing every which way off the ground and the branches as he slowly ascends beyond the treetops toward a rescue helicopter where Karl wonders if Irena is waiting.

He is on a sled, strapped in and wrapped in blankets. Or it could be a hammock or a bed, a giant pod or a cocoon, a crib or a cradle suspended in the stone-white sky above these woods and this countryside he loves. Had Sam asked even once, Karl would have described how sometimes the silver light of the star-lanes shines so luminescent you can see the shadows and the silhouettes of deer moving through long after nightfall. Through the interstellar dust of everything already dead millions of years and still falling back to us. Come see for yourself. That's all Karl ever meant to say: Yes, just stay here and talk to me. Please, stay here and be my son.

[The Dangerous Lay of the Land]

BARE-ARMED AND BARE-LEGGED in mid-February, Geneva is maybe a minute or two shy of the serious shivers and shakes. And Mr. Silvo, accidentally on purpose—or so she believes—has left the key in the ignition and, having returned to his classroom to make a phone call, is taking his sweet time getting out to her. He's been doing this more and more lately, testing not her road skills or her knowledge of the driver's manual, but rather what he deems to be her "impetuousness"—whatever that is.

As a consequence of the even-tempered and grown-up way that Mr. Silvo speaks to her, Geneva rarely flusters or turns panicky or indulges anymore in a tirade of obscenities. Neither did she get visibly pissed and—look, Ma, no hands—flip Lawson Ritt the double-barrel bird that day he tailgated tight to her ass and laid on his horn, flashing his headlights for her to pull over and let him pass.

Lawson Ritt is a nitwit. A loud-laughing, lost-cause high school dropout whose concerted efforts to repave every four-way-stop intersection in Chippewa County with burnt rubber defines, as Mr. Silvo maintains, the recklessness of a world gone mad. Road rage, he says. Hit-and-runs and rampant carjackings and bridges collapsing under the stress and fatigue of so much rush-hour traffic, sinkholes cavernous enough to swallow transport trailers whole. He says it's a veritable minefield out there, potential calamity lurking around every next bend, and the debris of human misery everywhere present and immense. This is why, guided by his calm and soft-spoken cautions, Geneva listens carefully and stays ever watchful, eyes on the road and both hands locked on the steering wheel as she's been taught.

Mr. Silvo's Subaru Outback doubles as the driver's ed car. It's got Oklahoma plates, which she finds curious, given that this is already his second year teaching English and music appreciation not forty miles south of Sault Ste. Marie on the Canadian border. A Sooner—that's what he once called himself. And later, when Geneva got out a Rand-McNally to better visualize where he was born and raised—the exact location—she fantasized about the two of them pushing hard across a half-dozen state lines to arrive there. Grain elevators and missile silos and unfamiliar road signs peppered with bird- or buckshot, and a take-what's-left motel room in another time zone when neither one of them can keep their eyes open anymore. Yet even in their exhaustion they'd stare wide-eyed out the car window at the full moon's illumination across those boundless acres of winter wheat—shimmering, she supposes, like ocean swells on the far side of the highway.

She has never ventured outside of Michigan, and her mom's metallic-red high-mileage wreck of a Mustang is so old it doesn't even have AC or an air bag or a catalytic converter. The license tags are already more than six months expired. But as her mom makes clear, that very same vehicle in showroom condition and her life waiting tables at Oney Jeez Roadhouse translate to ancient frigging history. Maybe so, Geneva thinks. Maybe knowing when to cash it in is always a matter of timing and foresight, of seeing that vanishing point *before* it vanishes, before it all goes up yet again in smoke.

Geneva's a senior, B-level grades as of this semester, and a B-cup.

She's grateful that Mr. Silvo did not know her as a flat-chested sopho-more, her hair high spiked and dyed a sheeny half-shade shy of an-tifreeze. The hair is fully back, as of the New Year, to her original raven black, and it's braided tight as a rope. Thanks be to her Ottawa blood—honest Injun, as her mom insists, yoo-hooing such ancestral nonsense whenever she's into the firewater, which means every time she soaks in their leaky third- or fourth-hand hot tub and watches the stars blur through the Smirnoff and the pain pills, her head tilted back, elbows hooked on the mildewed ledge, and the rez squeezed in too tightly around her. That's what the pale-faced pantywaists at school call it, as if Geneva and her mother sleep in teepees, decked out in loincloths and crow feathers and fancy Air Jordans after toking on a peace pipe to pass away the nowhere afternoons. The rez. She hates the handle and the taunt. She thinks, Lamebrains. Thinks, Gutless liars, every gas-bagging last one of them.

Yet under state police interrogation—a court-appointed attorney present—she admitted finally in a tear-burst confession to taking her first ever toke right there with Totem and Casey Beal, not naming names but nodding when certain ones were mentioned, among them both of these brothers whom she loved and trusted and who, as if guided by sign or premonition, boarded that very night a northbound Trailways to parts unknown, never to be heard from again. Oklahoma, Geneva calculates, might be the distance *she* needs to erase such a de-pressing history forever from her head.

So some nights she does dream of lighting out with Mr. Silvo, the radio cranked, the two of them on the loose and belting out the chorus of "Jersey Girl" or "Radar Love." But just last week, sitting in the pas-senger seat, he hadn't even bothered to buckle up, which was entirely out of character, and when she asked, "Where to?" he directed her to stop at the empty end of the school parking lot, the front bumper kiss-ing the chain-link, and there they sat, the engine idling, and chatted nonstop for the entire session. As if he were a caseworker, though he knew full well she'd finished with all of that, her probation over and no more mandatory urine tests, her attendance satisfactory after she was readmitted to school on a trial basis, and her GPA on the gradual up-climb. And most important, after all this time, a valid driver's license in her foreseeable future.

By Easter—that's the plan. May flowers to follow, and as far-flung as the notion sometimes sounds she nonetheless contemplates—on Mr. Silvo's recommendation—applying to college in Escanaba or Marquette. He says he believes in her. Says it a lot, and not in that grab-ass manner of certain grown men she's spent bad time around.

Only once has he mentioned his wife, Carly Roe Silvo. Not like it was their anniversary or anything. Just a typical Mr. Silvo sentence with a strange name in it. A nice-sounding one, Geneva thought, but his having said it aloud in front of her seemed to trigger in Mr. Silvo a deep-weird and eerie kind of faraway quiet, as if he were bracing for the predicted blizzard's full impact to slam them head-on. But it never arrived, and as they locked eyes for the first time ever in the rearview mirror, it was, to her surprise, he who turned away.

Early thirties is her guess, which makes him more her mom's age—thirty-three and counting—but the way he always drops Geneva off, at her request, a good quarter mile before the trailer park causes her throat to go silky. As if they're sneaking around, with her mom asking every Friday evening—accusing her, more like—"Oh, so you've started back with the cancer sticks?" A know-nothing remark, and Geneva simply shakes her head, revealing not a single detail about how Mr. Silvo, out of politeness, always asks, "Just say if this bothers you, okay?" before he nervously burns through half a pack of Chesterfields, the window cracked but only a hair, and the smoke-swirl hanging silvery blue and heavy all around them. The urge to light up is still killing her, and if it weren't for Mr. Silvo's assertion that a worthwhile life is a matter of willpower and fortitude and the wherewithal to follow through, odds are she would have somewhere succumbed. It's possible he's testing her on this front, too, so her every temptation to take that first slow drag is made almost sweet by the intense, hard-core torture of resisting it.

Geneva is not blind to the dangerous lay of the land, the self-destructive addictions of women and men. She's seen it all: her mom's last or next-to-last or next new boyfriend pulling up, wrecked on something, always after midnight, with his flywheel's high-idle whine like a needle's icy frequency throbbing nonstop from deep in her left eardrum to her temple and back. Early on, Geneva wanted to believe that, if ignored, these wannabe world-beaters would eventually go away.

But they didn't and they don't, not for long. Instead they just sit there as inert as crash dummies in their jacked-up Silverados or Dodge Power Wagons or rust-bucket Monte Carlos, laying claim to that same identical parking place for as long as it takes Geneva's mom to come rescue them—and for the sake of those lonely last motorists still out running the roads she *will*, half-dressed, leave the house and lead each one of them back inside to sleep it off in her bedroom. A continuous inventory of no-accounts not hard to imagine in handcuffs, although nine years have elapsed since the sheriff's department deputies last hauled anyone off, her mom's eye socket goring-up and her breastbone bruised while she yelled split-lipped at the top of her lungs, "Do you hear me? This shit is going to fucking stop, you bastard, goddamn you," and the cruiser's red-and-blue lights slapping hard against the warped and faded aluminum siding.

Geneva has not seen nor heard from her stepfather since, not following his release from prison or any time thereafter, but some nights she'll sit bolt upright in her bed, sweat-drenched in a tangle of sheets, and whisper, "Dear Jesus, merciful Almighty, oh, please, for the love of God, no," remembering how her stepfather would tiptoe into her room, rangy and lean and squinty-eyed, and hold a disposable lit butane so close to her face that she only ever nodded yes to whatever it was he would commence to do to her. Or force her to do for him. Even now, just thinking about him, she can feel her cheekbones ignite into flames.

Only out of malice or revenge has Geneva mashed lips with those clumsy, peach-fuzzed eager beavers whose jealous girlfriends used to freeze up tight at the very sight of her. Yes, *her*—that spacey, whacked-out half breed turned do-gooder, last seen leaving school today dressed as if it were Indian summer, the Stars and Stripes coming down from the flagpole, and those purple-blue bursts of school bus exhaust long dispersed into the atmosphere.

Geneva snaps to when Mr. Silvo *rap-raps* with his knuckles, his face so close to the safety glass that she can see his pupils dilated in the lusterless, indistinct, late-afternoon light. She hadn't noticed him coming out of the school or crossing the parking lot. But this is the excuse she needs to start the car, the heater set at full blast, and in the slow hum of the automatic window going down she smiles at him.

"I have to cancel," he says. "I'm sorry. Something's come up." But he doesn't specify what. He just stands there, his gloved hands tucked into his armpits while he quick-shifts from foot to foot, wearing his hand-knit tasseled scarf and a vest, and each thin breath cloud that rises turning the neatly trimmed edge of his mustache white.

Mr. Silvo's not blind—he can't be—to how badly this messes her up, and she'd rather not explain to him that it's her mom's turn to work a double shift, plus it's so bone-cold bitter outside. Besides, as he's well aware, the trailer park is ten miles out, and just last month their telephone service was interrupted again for nonpayment, and from day to day Geneva never really knows if it will ring when she calls home or if her mom will even bother to answer it. But that's a moot consideration since all Geneva has to do is exit the Subaru, expressionless except for that exposed flat midriff inch or two, and her limbs aquiver with chill bumps, to cause Mr. Silvo to shake his head in disbelief and ask, "Where in heaven's name is your coat?"

It's hanging up in her locker, right above her boots—the practical, fur-lined pair she traded into at Goodwill, straight up, for the shit-kickers harnessed in chains and silver studs that she used to wear, their heels scudding heavy as anvils down those big square-tiled, snot-green hallways. She hates being trapped in that mad-clatter, final-bell rush of the week, and so she'd sneaked out the side door—information she withholds and instead just shrugs and hugs herself, her teeth starting to chatter.

He says, "Never mind, I'll take you home. It's okay. Really, it's fine. It's all right. Come on, hop back in before you turn hypothermic." But then he pauses and says, "What were you thinking on a day like this?" But she stays closemouthed and he just nods, saying, "Doesn't matter." Then he says, "You drive," and just like that they're back in cruise mode—their labored breathing, she notices, in perfect sync.

Unlike those burnout teachers who arrive each morning already nerved up, glowering, and ready to pop, Mr. Silvo stays even-keeled, his voice never rising much above a whisper. Sometimes Geneva has to lean in toward him so as not to miss what he's saying. He's like that with everyone, always attentive and super nice. No negative vibes, not ever, and it makes her furious the way some of the students pantomime a demented, two-fingered "Heil Hitler" behind his back, and then smirk and nose-snigger like the piss-minded mouth breathers they are. Other times they'll play their invisible violins or refer to him as E.T. because of the way his right hand is missing the last two and a half fingers. A grain auger is one rumored version, but farm-raised doesn't from her vantage seem remotely feasible. Hay bales and pitchforks and all those milk-swollen udders to lubricate and squeeze? Uh-uh. No way can she imagine that, no matter where in the heartland he originated.

He's worldly, Mr. Silvo is. Courtly even, but not so much as to nullify maybe sometime playing stickball against the backstop satellite dish the Beal brothers excavated from the county landfill one summer and somehow hauled back to the trailer park. A primer-gray monstrosity with medicine big enough—as they used to tell her—to intercept soul signals beamed down from all the exiled tribes reunited in revenge, a news she'll never in the New World get wind of on Fox or CNN.

The Beal brothers are less than eleven months apart in age, and so by the numbers just two and three years older than Geneva. Tricksters, that's how she remembers them—tall, thin, hard-muscled lightning rods. Nobody to mess with, that's for sure, and she felt protected in their company, flanked by a brother on either side whenever they ranged outside the confines of the trailer park. Like she was their little sister, so any hooch-hounds sniffing around for pelvis and thatch ought first to consider the consequences: scalped or skinned alive by the Beal brothers, the finely honed blades in those hand-stitched, homemade leather sheaths strapped tight to their thighs.

Totem and Casey, who in their invisible feint and dodge to slip away had never even said good-bye or left a note or ever once got back in touch. And why would they after she'd sold them out the way she did, scared and confused and oblivious to the self-loathing she'd later feel. Each day she'd discover even fiercer ways to hate and hurt herself. A stool pigeon she was, a traitor so turncoat that her own face stared back viper-eyed from the deepest deep undergloom of the mirror whenever she dared turn on the bathroom light.

She misses the brothers and always has, and not for one single second in her longing has she ever lost sight of them. The way they'd howl and hoot each time they'd pop another Old Milwaukee and twist open their tins of Red Man and toast all the fringes of being Indian. "To you," they'd say, and cracking up all shit-and-giggles they'd clink cans to the great white treaty makers, the Mr. Kemo-fucking-sabes, as they war-danced around the trailer park, small dust clouds rising under the muted drumbeats of their feet. Geneva worries that if someday she were to pick up the brothers on an off-ramp while they were hitchhiking to some other next hideaway, they wouldn't recognize her from Eve.

The car's warning light's not on when she begins driving away from the school, but Geneva points to the fuel gauge anyway, the glow-green needle hovering midway between an eighth and empty. She's been warned that in single-digit temperatures such as these the threat of gas-line freeze is *palpable*, as Mr. Silvo always says.

She likes when he uses *p* words, the way she can almost feel them puff and pucker before being launched from his lips: *pertinacious*—that's one she remembered and looked up in the dictionary, but now she's forgotten what it means. And *Peugeot*, which he confided is the kind of car his wife drives, but that up here in the far northern reaches the design is all wrong, especially with the undercarriage offering too little clearance and making her more often than not afraid to go out alone. Too *perilous*, Geneva reasons—a vocabulary word from English Lit that she got right on last week's quiz and that on days like this defines to a T the wind-whipped road conditions, the shell-sculpted drifts and the whiteouts. But unlike Carly Roe, Geneva craves the high she gets from all that danger, especially on those long straightaways between the corn-stubble fields where sometimes, if no other cars are about, Mr. Silvo will slow-nod as she accelerates all the way to sixty-five, her heart racing faster and faster each time the engine slides into another gear, the all-wheel-drive Subaru floating ghostlike over those treacherous patches of hidden black ice.

Mr. Silvo shakes his head, shuts and then thumb-rubs his eyes with his knuckles, and says, "Simple absent-mindedness." Truth told, he has seemed more concentrated on other things, all of them lost to her during those interminable silences when he drifts so far away.

"Should never happen," he says. "Always check and then recheck just to be sure," an admonition addressed not to her for a change but to himself. He means, of course, the gas gauge, and she feels momentarily faint as he reaches over and resets the odometer, the last two fingers of his glove flopping loose from the others, ring and pinky, plus there's a sag where the meaty portion of the palm and heel used to be.

That glove is hard not to look at, as though it's a part of the DVD he sent home with her on day one. Not fender benders or whiplash but graphic footage of bodies and body parts, and cars so mangled and charred they had to be hoisted, some of them still smoking, onto flat-beds with a crane. So much carnage and mayhem that Geneva's mom muted the sound and, before abandoning her bowl of Fritos and sour cream dip to the floor, said, "Sweet Jesus on a crutch," as if even he, the Savior, couldn't walk away unscathed from something like that.

It's gruesome to contemplate, but nonetheless true, that a fatality occurs in this country every thirteen minutes, and most often at night, as Mr. Silvo has reminded her. What he calls *wrongful* deaths. Drivers usually under twenty-five, either booze- or drug-impaired, and so listen up—no filters, no beating around the bush—because he's speaking directly to the who that Geneva *was*, and not all that long ago, whenever he asks, "And how does someone then live with that?"

She doesn't know and tries not to dwell on it. What's now is all that matters—and Mr. Silvo agrees, "ultimately speaking," and he's not just another forked-tongued adult saying one thing but full of silent, condescending judgments to the contrary. He speaks what he believes: that she is both courageous and estimable, which she misheard that day as Istanbul, and only tracking backward later that night did she figure out that Turkey wasn't anywhere close to what he meant. He was complimenting her on how, ever since her arrest, she hasn't caved or taken even a single hit of hashish, her used-to-be drug of choice. Or pot, for that matter, or that next half line of coke so pure it always felt like a cool spring mist for that instant before the initial blood rush fine-sprayed from both nostrils and every nerve ending in her face went numb.

In less than two months she will turn eighteen, a legal adult, already a year and a half older than when her mom, on April 13, 1991, prematurely delivered a baby girl—four pounds, eight ounces, and that space on the certificate for the birth father's name left blank. An immaculate conception, as the doctor later joked. But look at Geneva's skin, her torrent of shiny black hair, "And go ahead, tell me I'm mistaken," as her mom harangues whenever the subject of a family tree beyond the two of them comes up. There are times when Geneva not only concocts the fantasy, but deep down believes that she was a switched or brokered baby, her name entirely misappropriated for this girl raised up here in the boonies by a forlorn and deadbeat single mom.

Mr. Silvo is all about quotas and need and scholarships, and he's offered to help Geneva fill out the forms and to advise her on which boxes to check. He says, contrary to what she's heard, that the members-only club *only* holds if she buys into such nonsense. There are ways, he says, that are affordable and fair, and in her case a full ride isn't out of the question. And no, she's definitely not, he often reassures her, learning disabled—a hasty and harsh and erroneous diagnosis if ever there was one—and so she can, now and forever, forget about that. She's plenty smart and, whatever it takes, a good education is the single best investment she'll ever make in her future. In this *country's* future, he says, but whatever that has to do with blood moons and ceremonial dances and what he calls "an alternate frame of reference," she's not sure. A more "indigenous worldview," he says, not intending to but making her feel like some matinee Pocahontas.

The one and only time Geneva mentioned college to her mom she was told, "Stop wishing off and get a job. There's that, you know. It's called the *real* world." And "Forgive my lack of faith in miracles, but part the waters my ass," her mom continued, already half shitfaced and climbing stark naked out of the hot tub, her arm outthrust. "This is who we are. Go ahead, deny it all you want, but the short end of the goddamn stick is what we're holding and always have been."

Then she mumbled something about glitter and eye shadow and about all the brainless young Marilyns; her own bottle-blond locks had gone stringy and dark orange at the roots. "Look around you," her mom said, dripping wet and suddenly louder and clumsy-stumbling and fighting back sobs, the double-wide half trashed and everything pawnable long ago cashed out for quarters and dimes. Then she was opening a drawer, reaching in, and waving a fistful of scratch-offs and yelling, "Why can't you come to your senses for once? You don't start helping out around here . . ." But she didn't finish, except to ask, "Do you understand a single word of what I'm saying? Answer me, Geneva. Do you?"

Yes, she does. All except for the secret excitement that she entertains for a clingy chemise and satin sheets and the right man so eager to please that he makes her light-headed and wet between the legs.

But the truth is that Geneva feels no rise or flutter as she sits parallel to the pumps at the BP mini-mart where Mr. Silvo has had her stop and where it has started to flurry—though not densely enough to obscure Mr. Silvo, his thin shoulders low-slung against the unrelenting bomb blasts of subarctic cold. Geneva watches him in the side-view mirror, his eyes closed as he slowly rotates his head left and then right, as if trying to pop loose a kink in his neck. He's looked battle-weary lately, his face gone puffy and the whites of his eyes flecked red. Sick sleep, she calls it, all restless tossing, an affliction she knows plenty about. That and those dildos at school—their meanness and mocking. No wonder Mr. Silvo's breathing turns quavery now whenever he speaks, the wind gusts unloading on him from every direction making it impossible to cover up and duck away.

There must be a word for somebody like him, who never complains and who sometimes during a lull in their conversation will point and then recite the Latin names of scrub trees unpronounceable to her. She's all but hypnotized by the sounds the extended vowels make and by the way he magically calms himself saying them in song. Like a chant echoing up from beneath this hardpan of mined-out copper and iron ore and standing beech and oak stumps the size of giant wooden washtubs.

Jerkwater town, her mom calls it. The absolute pits and, no pun intended, home to one decent-sized meteor crater geologists sometimes still visit with their Geiger counters. Not much else, though. The foundry long closed and gutted, all the windows busted out and the wind and snow blasting through like buzz bombs, the population declining with each new census. But mention leaving, and the wrongness in that causes something in Geneva's brainpan to short-wire. She'll say, "Where to? Which way, exactly?" As if every dream or road or river out doubled back on itself and ended up right here at the trailer park: the doorjambs narrow and the drop ceilings low enough to reach up and touch; wallboard most anybody could punch through with a balled fist, the evidence in virtually every room impossible to miss.

Because winter has descended again, her mom's back on the warpath with the gas company, attempting to forestall payment of that next preposterous, impossible-to-cover bill. Always the exact same rant about how she's been bagged and swindled and jacked around long enough. And about how the steaming hot tub cools down slower than anywhere inside their double-wide, and have they ever, for one greedy second, considered that? "Slower by far," she says, and pending further notice she swears to Christ and Christopher Columbus that she'd rather paint her body red and die in her birthday suit out there with a last drink in tow than apply to the state as a goddamn hardship case and for all she cares hell itself can freeze the fuck over. This is the same kind of borderline cuckoo talk that led to custody issues shortly after the stepfather's arrest, though in the end the woman judge showed mercy enough not to foster Geneva away to Brightside as a ward of the state.

The Subaru's heater is blowing waves of hot, dry air nonstop from under the dash, up under her skirt and all the way to the waistband, making her want to recline the seatback, kick off her shoes, and stare out at what little grayish-green light still lingers in the winter sky. But Mr. Silvo, she notices, is signaling with his free hand for her to get out of the car, and two steps before she reaches him he says, "Here, take these," and he hands her his gloves, his scar a glutinous purplish color under the buzzing fluorescent overheads.

"If you help me this will take only a minute," he says, the nozzle already back in the pump, the gas cap twisted on. He's tugging at the tie-downs, saying, "Hold on a sec." Then he loosens his hold and re-grabs the strap from another angle and says, "Okay, try lifting when I yank," and abracadabra she's suddenly cradling the yellow-and-black STUDENT DRIVER sign, its metal heft burning like dry ice against the soft, bare skin of her forearms.

"Here, let me take that," he says. "You get back in the car. Rider's side." He opens and then slams the rear hatch closed; he blows into his cupped hands, rubbing them together, the dismembered one dwarfed by the other.

"Don't you want your gloves?" she asks, but he's already got his wallet out, a credit card squeezed between his index finger and thumb, like pincers. "Thank you, I'm fine," he says. Hunched over, he half walks, half skates his way to the mini-mart entrance, his baggy brown wide-wale corduroys flapping like wind socks. Geneva can hear the bell jingle when the glass door opens, and she can see Mr. Silvo pointing back outside and then up at the wall grid of cigarette packs behind the counter.

Her coordination has, at best, only halfway returned by the time he slides behind the wheel, an unlit Chesterfield between his lips. But before *he* can do it, Geneva pushes the lighter in, and every space inside her goes instantly tingly, like a sudden spray of tiny stars. Or like champagne, she thinks. She has never acted so forward with him before, so impulsively, and she's close to some flash point when he turns, full focus, and stares directly at her.

One one-thousand, two one-thousand, three . . . is all her mind can muster until he says, just short of a whisper, "Is there any certain time you need to be home?"

"No," she says, higher-pitched than she intends.

Since her curfew's been lifted she's free to come and go. The reason he asks, he says, is because he has one important stop to make if that's all right. "It's in the opposite direction and might take a while," he says, but her single, consenting, slow-motion nod assures him that she's got no other plans for the night, not a single other place on this frozen planet to be. Besides, she likes his company, and he hers—and what, anyway, is so wrong with that? They haven't done anything. Mr. Silvo has never once come on to her. Never undressed her with his eyes or soft-stroked her cheek or hair or said a single inappropriate thing. Not even close, and she needs no advice on what her mom calls "catting around."

Not when it comes to Mr. Silvo. "Thank you, but no, I'm not hungry," she tells him when he asks, and who eats at normal hours anyhow? Nobody in a two-person, TV-tray household like hers. Not to mention that the doggy-bag lamb shank and succotash specials her mom's bad habits drag home every Friday night congeal and intensify Geneva's craving to stay gone for as long as she possibly can. Home is always empty and cold, all pipey with clanks so loud the entire trailer park sounds as though it were freezing solid, with the bare light bulbs dimming in their thin copper sockets and every battery in every beater exploding like hand grenades under the hoods.

"Tchaikovsky's Piano Trio in A Minor," Mr. Silvo says, sliding in a CD and pulling out past Payless and the Pretty Good Grocery, heading west on 665 toward Brimley and Bay Mills, his right index finger lilting back and forth like a baton, the master of ceremonies, but his elbow stone-steady on the armrest between them.

The trio is a far reach from her tomahawk rendition of "Chopsticks" on a shiny, lacquered-black baby grand that night she and the Beal brothers raided a house for liquor and then howled their drunken concertos out the open windows of the pickup they hot-wired and then abandoned grill-deep in a bog they hit full-speed and almost careened across. "Almost," Totem said.

Geneva judges them to be three, maybe four miles beyond the town limits when Mr. Silvo lowers the volume and asks her to grab a blanket from the back seat. It's a simple request, and the only reason she momentarily balks is because it reminds her of driving in the Mustang with her mom, a scratchy, worn-out Tanya Tucker tape in the deck and Geneva bent forward scraping thin ribbons of ice off the windshield from the inside with her fingernails. A bad thermostat, and instead of getting it repaired, her mom's temporary, already two-year-old quick fix is a ratty wool Hudson Bay stinking of mothballs.

Geneva wonders if tonight's excursion will culminate with Mr. Silvo turning off the heat. It can't be much above zero outside, and that single tower flame fluming skyward from the natural gas well appears half-frozen above the otherwise empty expanse of snowfield backlit with its scrim of pinkish light. She figures that a simulated breakdown beyond walking range of any rescue could, as crazy as it sounds, be what Mr. Silvo's got in mind. Always the teacher, emergency rations and distress flares no doubt stashed somewhere in the back.

"That's it," he says, as she lifts the blanket, carefully folded, onto her lap. "Now go ahead and wrap it around you."

She does what he tells her, though he gives no indication of pulling over and killing the engine, or even slowing down. Maybe he should. He's already fishtailed a couple of times, as if minus the driver's ed sign equals a different car and driver, but more likely he's just late—hurrying, Geneva speculates, to wherever he's scheduled to pick up his kids. That is, of course, if he has any. She wouldn't mind babysitting some night for them if he does. He's never said and she's never inquired, but she thinks he'd make the perfect father.

Just ahead, the road shadows the river in a kind of double snake trail into the snow, which is falling faster and rooster-tailing up like a smoke screen behind the Subaru. They've never driven out in this direction, so she feels momentarily disoriented, mesmerized by the vortex of millions of miniature white galaxies tunneling slow-motion into the headlights like something out of *Star Wars*.

"On the floor right behind you," Mr. Silvo says, "there's a pair of binoculars. Grab those for me, too, if you would."

They're weighty and long barreled, fat and wide at the ends, and she's clueless as to what anyone could possibly make out on a night like this, the visibility worsening by the minute. Except, of course, though she won't say it, the county dump, where black bears in late summer are occasionally sighted, and where those tone-deaf, know-nothing snarks who make fun of Mr. Silvo guzzle beer and listen to scores of bullets ripping holes through the darkness.

It's all of a sudden *too* warm with the blanket draped around her, and now that Mr. Silvo has ejected the CD, she can hear the paper of his cigarette burning. He's sucking that hard on it, his blinker on, and before she can see that there's a road there, he hooks a turn and skids sideways to a stop, not burying the front bumper in the snowbank, but close.

At first she thinks he has, the way the headlights go dark and the visible universe draws closed around them. Then it dawns on her that he's turned them off. For a few long seconds she's unaware that the car is still moving, but once her eyes adjust she can make out the feature-less, whitewashed woods slipping past, and Mr. Silvo concentrating nowhere except on that next few feet of snowy road directly ahead.

"We're just about there," he says. "We're close. A few more min-utes is all." But those minutes come and go, and then a few more, before Geneva can see what appear to be house lights, their faint ra-diance diminishing and pulsing. She thinks of candles, and then of someone slowly flicking through signed-off TV channels—that static she sometimes wakes to, like the soft shaking of castanets, and finds her mom, still wearing her waitress uniform, passed out cold on the couch.

They're almost halfway around what appears to be a narrow, high-banked cul-de-sac when Mr. Silvo stops again. He shifts into reverse and, backing into a driveway, reaches up and pushes a button on the visor. An overhead garage door opens behind them. Nobody in her trailer park even has a garage, unless fudging a carport counts, and a single halogen sentry on a corroded pole is as fancy as the lighting there gets. Mr. Silvo doesn't have even that to steer by here, so he has to put down his window and lean out into the cold to make sure he doesn't miscalculate and ass-end the rear wall. Geneva has yet to at-tempt this maneuver, and she wonders why he's demonstrating it for her way out here, smack-dab in the heart of another midwinter storm.

He warned her weeks ago about the danger of accidental carbon monoxide deaths—kids like her in headsets closing their eyes. But Geneva is wide awake, and the only music now is the sound of the engine ticking and cooling down as Mr. Silvo gathers half the blanket around him and presses the binoculars tight to his eyes, the garage door suspended above them. Time itself has stopped, the night as thick and dark as India ink.

Could be the binoculars are those fancy infrareds, but why would he be spying—and on who? The moment is borderline spooky when he says, "Carly Roe," as if he's reading Geneva's mind.

"That's our house. That's where we live," he says, though even squinting hard she can't see anything, not so much as an outline. "This one here, this house—the garage we're in? It belongs to the McKenzies, a retired couple. I look after it for them while they're away in Arizona. But out here's fine. We don't need to go inside. We won't be here long enough—not in this weather."

While Mr. Silvo fine-focuses, the drowsy light of a picture window begins to widen for Geneva right there across the way, blue tinged like a glacier. Even bare-eyed, she can see what she's certain is a human form, wavy and blurred like those underdeveloped Polaroid self-portraits, so bleached out that only she can tell who's staring back, who it is that belongs to those phantom, deep-set acetate eyes.

Maybe she's hallucinating. The way Casey Beal said he did for months after some Indian haters from the next town over, all fake-friendly and asking directions, threw quicklime in his eyes and peeled away, their boozy victory whoops hanging in the air above him. He explained how after he gagged back the crying and shaking and stood stock-still—Indian-style—the sky and mountains far away turned the color of belladonna, and the hazy clouds shimmered like pure white forests. Casey was only eight years old and possibly blind for good— the emergency doctor's diagnosis—though in the end only time would tell. And his dad, on the drive home from the hospital, describing a mystical landscape in native words Casey had never heard but still understood, his sweaty palms cupped around his blistered lids to staunch that white-hot burning.

"We're just in time. Here. Have a look," Mr. Silvo says, and when Geneva does, the magnified flakes grow huge and glow like orbs of phosphor, the snow magically tapering back again to flurries, and a woman so close up that Geneva believes she can hear the sounds the bow makes moving slow-motion across the strings, can *almost* from this angle make out the individual notes of sheet music right there on the stand, and could reach over when this woman nods and turn the page for her.

"Cello," Mr. Silvo says. "Since the accident, it's the only time she plays anymore, every Friday evening before I get home." Then he says something about the complex repertoire of human grief, and how he used to be Carly Roe's accompanist. "Philadelphia," he says. "Boston. Seattle. The Outer Banks one time"—all places as foreign to Geneva as Mars or the Mall of America, where her mom promised they'd visit but they never did. Like every other hope, that one turned hoax in her memory.

"A benefit concert in Prague," he says. "Three shows. That's where we fell in love." The roses he describes piled high on the floor outside Carly Roe's dressing room turn from red to pure white in Geneva's imagination.

"The hand has twenty-seven bones." That's what Mr. Silvo says next, and Carly Roe's are all moving up and down the long wooden neck of the cello, but Geneva cannot take her eyes off the woman's face. It's badly scarred—whether skin-grafted or burned Geneva can't tell for certain—but beautiful in the way the head cants slightly downward, and the hair is auburn and wavy and shoulder length, and the earrings glitter like mica.

A glimpse is all Geneva gets, and then another squall leaves everything blurred again and vacant.

"Ship to shore," he says. When he takes out his cell phone and dials, he presses his index finger to his lips, as if Geneva might shout out to Carly Roe for an encore, a final tune for all the travelers lost or stranded or father-orphaned at birth. For the runaways and for the stay-at-homes, those sounds of sorrow that Mr. Silvo one time said can define for us the music of beauty.

That song. Play *that* one, Geneva thinks. Right now, when no one is around or listening.

FOR ALL THAT MY DAD lost in his life, he was lucky at pure chance: raffles, bingo, drawings for food baskets. It was that way beating stoplights, too, and finding parking spots downtown on shopping nights, time always left on the meter. I remember how, in a long line for a Sunday matinee at the Victory Theater, he stepped to the glass booth, me beside him, and he said, "One adult, one kid," and then the ticket window closed behind us, the show sold out. I always believed that if he'd been in the war, men marching directly in front and in back of him would have been killed by sniper fire, or by mortars exploding through the roof of a mess hall tent just moments after he'd vacated.

The very day after I turned sixteen I got my driver's license. On those nights that I borrowed the car, I'd pick him up outside the carbide plant where, for months, he'd been working twelve-hour shifts, most of the money gone in advance to cover my mom's mounting medical bills. There was perpetual fire free-floating in the sky above the stacks, and that part of the lot where I parked was always in nightshade or shadows. "Don't make me wait," he said, and he said it one time and one time only. "No two ways about it. I walk out, I want to see you right here. Period." And so to be on the safe side, I provided myself plenty of leeway.

Sometimes I'd tune in stations as far distant as Milwaukee. Away from the daylight, as my dad would say, as if Wisconsin wasn't right across on the opposite side of Lake Michigan, but rather on the whole other side of the world. Other times I'd just close my eyes and drift awhile inside my head, and suddenly there he'd be, opening the car door, lunch pail in his free hand. "Come on, slide over. I'll drive," he'd say. That and not a whole lot else. At least not until we'd hear the Northern Pacific's blurry whistle, and then he'd quick-glance over at me, and he'd say, "Hang on, Sy." And he'd punch the gas down that straightaway toward the railroad crossing, where two red lights alternated their emphatic warning like giant, frantic, shiny glass heartbeats.

"Dad," I'd say, as the heavy wooden arm descended from the dark sky. So close to the windshield that I believed the station wagon actually ducked a few inches as we slid under, the car's suspension loose and bouncing and then fishtailing beyond the rails until finally we'd come to a sideways stop on the gravel road, the flywheel whining.

"Hallelujah," he'd say. "Damn near misjudged that one, but hey, another ten minutes saved," like we had some life-depending deadline to meet. "But don't you go breathing one word of this to your mother—she'll skin us alive," he said, as if, by implication, I was somehow responsible too. Like father, like son. "And don't *you* ever attempt this, no matter what. You hear me?" And speechless I'd simply nod, as if here or anywhere in God's creation I'd want to start my own heart walloping in my chest like that.

One Labor Day, before we left for the county fair I studied the racing forms for hours, and, aided by Carl Yezbak's FAVORITE PICKS from the newspaper, I narrowed and narrowed the field, certain that even against impossible odds I'd picked all nine winners. Not a single one finished in the money. My dad, locking the car in the quack grass lot of someone's front yard, had simply jotted down the last two digits from the odometer, played those numbers, and collected $198.80 on the Daily Double. "It's all about attraction. Like tack nails to a magnet," he said. "Either you possess it or you don't." And to prove his theory, he thumbnail-flipped a shiny copper Depression penny he always carried in his change purse, higher and higher into the air. "Heads," he said. "Head's again." And then tails three times in succession, as if however he called it determined some new physics by which the coin was destined to land.

If he attended a Ducks Unlimited dinner in Graying or Kalkaska, he'd walk away with the most coveted prize sure as shooting. One year an electric smoker, next year a Remington 12-gauge pump, which at full choke smacked, as he put it, the stuffing out of migrating Snows at over a hundred yards. At first I thought he meant a shotgun powerful enough to turn back winter, but he just stared at me with that wracked, confused expression and said, "Geese, Sy. We're talking waterfowl and velocity." And like he sometimes did, he tapped my forehead, like knock-knock, is the toad up there anywhere in the pond? I didn't say so, but swim in my dreams and nobody's setting decoys or sky-busting along the flyways. As much as he wanted me to hunt with him I never did anymore, and he hadn't asked in a long time. Field-dress it quick as you can was his standing "motto," but I detested that hot, fresh-kill musk smell of wild game, and how it would permeate my clothes, and even worse how it lingered forever on my hands. At school I'd keep them fisted in my pockets, "tormenting the trouser mouse," as my best buddy, Billy Pipes, would babble and clown.

I guess I shouldn't have been surprised when, the very same week that my dad got transferred back to days, he won the giant Christmas Giveaway. An all-expenses-paid trip to Hawaii, to Molokai, where he'd be guided on a boar hunt. Not penned-up pigs busted loose and turned feral in the woods and swamps behind our house, but rather that sharp-tusked, high-backed native species born into the wild to maim and gore. "Cash it in, Milt. We can use the money," is what my mom said. "Some choicer scraps to ring in the New Year, which just might be an adventure for all of us."

I'd once raised a heifer for 4-H. A "beefcritter," as my dad referred to it, and that fall I watched as he touched the steel-blue muzzle of a .22 to that small bull's-eye hollow behind its ear, and when he fired, froth burst from both nostrils like two crimson water bombs. I doubled-over and retched for a good half hour, as if attempting to disgorge my own insides. Then again as I cut through the belly hair and hide, wiping my mouth and silently cursing my dad. Gun-shy all that fall in his presence, I'd flinch at his slightest movement or his raised voice, even though I trusted deep down that he wasn't an evil or violent man. Impetuous, unpredictable, but equally quick to order his thoughts, and to calm and compose himself if need be in the private or the public eye.

I was too young to recall, but I'd heard the rumors, and although I wanted in the worst way for them to be either denied or corroborated, it wasn't until years after the alleged altercation that he confessed to me. Short version: the trial-by-jury judge had denied into evidence the rattail file that my dad had used to stab some hog-head bully intent on fist-whipping a woman half his size. "And not to put too fine a point on it," he said, and winked at me, "but the son of a bitch, he deserved a goddamn stake through the heart." It's not by any calculation the only time he'd been in trouble, but as far as I'm aware he never spent even a single night in jail, so I guess he was lucky in that way, too.

His favorite singer was Julio Iglesias, whose top-forty hits my dad would slow-whistle to death whenever he grilled venison steaks and chops and brats outside, no matter the weather. Which was travelers advisory that morning I drove alone with him three hours south to the Grand Rapids airport, the voice on the weather station straining through heavy crackle and static. Whorls and a few whirlwinds and whiteouts, but no pileups or big rigs jackknifed across the highway, so we made okay time, my dad white-knuckled and silent and hunched forward over the steering wheel the entire way. When we arrived flights were being canceled left and right, but he just grabbed his bag from the rear seat and said, "Don't wait around in case the roads get any worse. Go slow you'll be fine, and if you need them—the tire-chains—they're right there in the far back with the jumper cables."

"What if *you* get stranded?" I said, and he just smiled like he was on roll. All spades and sunshine and pissing champagne, as Billy Pipes always insisted. "Your dad," he'd say. "Hell's bells, he plays Vegas one time, just fathom your immediate net worth." It's not like that, I'd tell him, the endless, flat space of the snow expanding as the winds whipped down from Canada each night, across the Straits toward us and the temperatures plummeting to sub-zero.

Not the best time for him to be away, but it was now or never and factor in all that OT, both at work and on the home front to take care of my mom, and any resentment from either of us seemed both selfish and small-minded.

"Here," he said, and leaned in and handed me a crisp twenty for gas and snacks, then he shook my hand, which he never, ever did. "Stay close to home," he said. "And drive your mother wherever she needs to be. Understood?" he asked, but before I could even answer he disappeared back into the terminal, the sliding glass doors closing tightly behind him.

By Friday a postcard arrived—a gorgeous, dark-haired Polynesian woman naked to the waist, her nipples barely concealed by cursive, sunny-yellow aloha letters, no matter which way I tipped and tilted the image, her rear end lifted high and her right thigh sticking out from a grass skirt. On the reverse side not a reminder for my dad's scheduled downstate arrival time, but instead a single dried thumb-print of blood.

I opted against showing it to my mom, who'd ceased being well when I was maybe eleven or twelve, though the wheelchair-access ramp to the front door had only recently been installed. It's not that she couldn't walk with a cane or, on her better days, even plug in the cord and slowly vacuum the living room. But a fall the previous winter had fractured her hip, so we weren't taking any chances, her bones appearing more fragile and exposed with every next disappearing pound she shed. Osteoporosis. That was the diagnosis, her sweaters pooching-up higher and higher in the shoulders and elbows. Try guessing her age, you'd overshoot by a long ways, and my dad still agile and youthful-looking and, unlike her, still wearing his wedding band. No chance a stranger would ever guess them to be man and wife, but consider the patient, soft-spoken tone he always used to talk to her and I swear love anywhere else pales by comparison.

Most nights she'd doze off in the cold blue light of the TV, and my dad—he'd bend down and kiss her cheek or temple and whisper, "Lydia, wake up. Time for bed," and he'd all but carry her up to the landing, where she'd hold tight to the newel post for another interminable few seconds before taking those last half-dozen tentative steps on her own. For that reason alone I selfishly hoped he'd change his mind and stay so that *I* wouldn't have to assist her in that way. "No," she said when I offered. "I'll sleep right here on the pullout while your father's away sipping highballs by the sea." And we both smiled at such a notion, faraway and impossible to honestly conceive. I got out the sheets and blankets, her pillow and nightgown from upstairs. The couch unfolded easier than I anticipated, and I slid a couple of coasters under the stocky, square iron bed legs so as not to leave any scars in the carpeting.

In fact, the most I had to do in addition to that was hold open her mitten cuffs for her to slide her hands inside. Then fasten the buttons on her coat and drive into town and push the shopping cart down the aisles of the IGA while she signaled from her wheelchair what provisions we needed to get us through the week. Van Camp's pork and beans, and a cut-rate party pack of cold cuts and a jar of beet pickles for my dad for when he got home. Plus some popcorn, which she said she wanted to string and drape on the Christmas tree. I knew that she couldn't, even if we salvaged one of those few remaining blue spruces abandoned on the lots and now free for the taking. Just one year earlier I'd arrived home late from school on the final day before vacation to the village of miniature skaters and carolers reveling under those lowest boughs in festive, hand-painted holiday attire. Plus tinsel spread so evenly on the branches that I imagined her separating each shiny silver strand between thumb and forefinger, and the pitch and needles making the house smell fresh like the out-of-doors.

My dad, prior to his departure, managed a wreath for the front door, complete with a red bow and fake, oversized candy canes. In holiday spirit I tried playing Bing Crosby's "White Christmas," but the turntable kept slowing like somebody somewhere was siphoning off our power. I even turned on the outside spots but the electric line to our house hadn't, to my eye, bowed any lower, and the window candles glowed halo-bright like they were supposed to. All the same I worried about a possible outage or a lockdown storm, and my dad, who was supposed to call across all those time zones, didn't. And my mom and me, we never once left the house after dark.

There was a ladder to the roof, which didn't yet need shoveling, and on a clear night every December you could just barely make out the angel wings spread wide on top of the water tower a mile or so distant. The population—2,069—was painted in white numerals across the front, but you'd need daylight and a high-power spotting scope to read those.

My dad claimed he'd climbed it once just to get that much closer to the stars. To make a wish, I figured, and what better place than way up there above the town? I liked that image of him a lot. But when I proposed to Billy Pipes that the two of us give it a go, he said, "Only a dildo would perform a stunt like that, Sy." And, he wanted to know, hadn't we pledged to hang around in this one life of ours long enough to at least get laid? "Our turn's about due," he said, but the closest I'd ever gotten was watching Jeannine Capinski's backside outflung for that half second it took her to slide into the desk seat in front of me in third period. Billy said he wished we owned a blowgun and darts that would stun young virgins into coveting *our* desires, and I quick-quipped that the odds of my dad smuggling back such contraband might actually be pretty decent.

The plane arrived right on time. He was the first one off, all sun-dark and still garlanded with a flower lei, and when he saw me wave, he ducked to one side and crouched real low on the sloping red carpet. Then, glancing back and forth, he sighted down the length of his empty arms and squeezed the imaginary trigger, his whole body jolted by the recoil. He stood up smiling, raised one finger, and I knew that it had been a perfect shot.

Outside it was still gray after the night's freezing rain and snow, but at baggage claim my dad was talking volcanoes and Dole's pineapples and Pearl Harbor, cockfights in a crowded garage. "Yessireebob," he said, and joked about where were the welcome banners and the writers from *Sports Afield* and *Outdoor Life*, his elbow on my shoulder, while he easy-tapped one boot toe as if keeping the rhythm to some island tune still playing in his head.

He hadn't leaned on me this way since we'd ceased hunting together, and that suddenly seemed like a long time ago. "Holy smokes, the tusks, you wouldn't believe, Sy. Upcurved like scythes," he said. "Razor-sharp. Hair bristled and coarse as burlap and body shapes like small bison." And I don't know why but I imagined the world suddenly pitched sideways when the conveyor belt clicked on. "See for yourself," he said. But instead of handing me a snapshot he just kept nodding, like any second now the boar might come rampaging right through those thick black rubber strap-flaps, knocking aside suitcases and baby strollers and whatever else threatened its bloodshot, wild-eyed escape into this foreign and frozen Michigan landscape.

"You mean you brought it back?" I asked, and he nodded again, like that'd be the sensible thing don't you think? Had he actually asked, I might have said, "I guess," but after another half an hour passed and I put two and two together, it became clear to me that the boar was lost in Portland, where my dad had changed planes on a tight connection. He said little, a detail here and there. And for what seemed like forever, he deadpanned away into some indiscernible middle distance, as if to picture the crate circling and circling in the humdrum of families chattering and flipping plastic name tags, sorting and stacking bags and boxes, and army-green canvas duffel bags from soldiers on leave. I prayed silently at that moment that the crate might still wind its slow way to where we waited, all alone now, and my dad's stare firmly fixed the way I'd seen it whenever we lost mallards or black ducks. Cripples that dove under and down into the muck and weeds and never came up. Or that buck he shot with a bow, an eight-point that we tracked for half a day but never found. Although I didn't say anything I figured the message hit home nonetheless when I flung the last of the toilet paper roll hard against a tree trunk marking where the blood trail stopped.

"Not for the goddamn life of me," he said, and I thought, Okay so here's where he comes unraveled, and he sort of did. "Blam-blam-blam," he said real loud as he pantomimed shooting up the place—the walls and ceiling tiles, the fluorescent tubes that buzzed nonstop above us.

"They'll find it," I said, and he just shot me a sidelong glance, like what did I know about that? I'd never boarded a plane, and this, the farthest south I'd ever been, seemed the unlikeliest and most unfamiliar place on the entire face of the earth.

"Good Christ Almighty. This is beyond belief, Sy. Come on, follow me," he said, and we headed for the escalator to the main concourse. Where I hoped there'd be a pay phone so I could call my mom and tell her don't wait up for us, given how it was already dark outside. And that things had misfired pretty badly but that we'd be home safe and sound as soon as we sorted some stuff out.

Instead we headed right for American Airlines, where half the passengers were filling out forms for lost luggage. No shoving or yelling, but nobody too pleased, either. And the agents scrambling to assist as ably as they could, though I figured it would be touch and go when it came to my dad, who surprised me by stepping quietly to the rear of the line. As calm as you please, as if we resided only a few miles up the road and no big deal, we could check back anytime tomorrow. And yes, thank you, the game shooting *was* worth all that time and travel.

But when the blond woman emerged from the back room and came onto the floor with her official blue blazer and gold wings and clip-board, I knew that no excuse or apology or explanation could mollify or account for what had occurred.

She handed my dad a sheet of paper with maybe fifty miniature suitcases in rows like stacked coffins or tombstones, each with a code at the center: A-10 or B-6, or C-3. A kind of X-ray picture I imagined hidden and magically exposed beneath the neatly folded towels and balled socks and underwear. My dad recognized nothing on the chart that resembled his cargo, and still scanning the sameness of the different diagrams, he said, "Pig."

"I'm sorry, what was that?" she said, her ballpoint cocked as if ready to impale the appropriate box.

"Pig," he repeated, like it was the only word he knew. Much louder this time, and a few people up ahead turned around as though he'd just accused his girlfriend or wife of having flown off to paradise for a fling with another man.

Maybe she ascribed to "pig" a brand name, or perhaps pig leather because she simply wrote it down, moved the pen tip to question number two and asked, "Color?"

I thought, How impossible to describe the bruised, filmy, vein-swirl pigment of any animal without its skin, and my dad stone-faced and seething, and people sidling out of range of him.

"I flew nine thousand air miles to shoot a wild boar. It's gone. Van-ished."

Boar appeared to make all the difference, passengers abandoning their places in line and forming a circle around him, and some guy yelling out at no one in particular, or at everyone to make his point, "How the hell can you lose a pig?"

I thought then of that chant in *Lord of the Flies* when the kids, crazed and crazy in war paint, return to camp shouting, "Kill the pig. Cut her throat. Spill her blood," the primitive ritual of the hunt a re-vival. Within minutes the entire tribe of travelers was astir. Savages in suit coats and wing tips and new oversized Hawaiian shirts. And one white-haired woman shooting the frenzy with her Polaroid, print after print spread out in a line on the counter. Even the agents crowded in to watch each next one develop under the harsh white lights, as if expecting the background to turn lush and green and tropical, and the boar carried on a long pole on the shoulders of two bare-chested porters. But all they saw was my dad in stop-time, shaking his fist against Delta and Pan Am and TWA and United, and most of all against American Airlines for ruining his return.

They put us up that night at the Hilton, plus a bottle of champagne that my dad drank much too fast in his bed, the bubbles rising non-stop like millions of tiny moons from the bottom of his plastic glass. While he talked with my mom, I turned down the volume on the TV so that I could listen to him reconstruct the events that had stranded us here.

"All I got is a pair of pants and a shirt to put on," he said, and when he inventoried the contents of what he'd lost, he never so much as mentioned the boar. In the lamplight his beard stubble appeared gray, the crow's-feet under his eyes like tiny road maps, and on the screen two kung fu warriors kept pummeling each other with knees and elbows and shinbones and not so much as a mark inflicted on either one of them.

"On the house," my dad said. "Soon. Tomorrow afternoon I'd guess." And no "nothing excuses nothing," but that at least the weather was predicted to break our way. "And you, you're holding up okay?"

Followed by some silence, during which he raised his glass and toasted me when he caught my eye, and then he said to my mom, "Call in sick for me first thing. For Sy, too," and I inclined a show of approval with a few on-the-spot kung fu moves of my own. My dad smiled at that and within a few minutes of hanging up his eyelids drooped and then closed and I reached over and lifted the half-empty glass from his hand and set it on the nightstand between us. I was tempted to take a sip but I didn't, and, still wide-awake, I switched off the TV and the lamp, and lay there on my back, staring into the dark, my dad's breathing even and slow. And what I hoped for most was that after I fell asleep, I'd wake up to sunshine and we'd order some bacon and eggs and orange juice, a short-stack of pancakes. Room service and no jet trails in the high blue of the sky on our ride home. No reminders of where my dad had been. Just an uneventful few hours until we pulled up in front of the house, everything back again to normal, everything around us intact.

The next afternoon my dad drove the station wagon right back among the planes refueling, escorted by one of those baggage jeeps, two square red flags streaming on the front fenders like on a hearse. The guy we followed was older than my dad and he wore a black watch cap pulled low to his eyes, and earphones against the thunder of aircraft. He parked parallel to a loading dock, jumped out, and directed us with one of those long-coned flashlights as though our 1964 Ford Fairlane was a DC8 swinging in a slow taxi off the runway.

We'd wanted to get an early start but already the day was sliding away. And my dad, opening the car door, said something about a jet stream that I didn't quite get, but I looked up anyway into the gray drizzle that hadn't been forecast.

"All set?" he said, finger-tipping the steering wheel. The recently replaced tailgate was hard to open, and so I knew without being asked to climb in back and kick from the inside while he held up on the latch. A derelict job is what my mom called the repair, and the way the guy looked at us I surmised that he thought so too.

"This your pig?" he yelled, pointing to a wooden crate, the other hand cupped around his mouth as if trying to be heard over the noise of the planes, though none were taking off right then or landing.

My dad, still hung over, shook his head. "Yeah," he said, as in, *You do the math.*

"Okay, let's lower her down," the guy said, and when we tipped the crate, a filmy, bluish liquid leaked out from the corner seams. "Probably spoiled," the guy shouted into my dad's face as they wrestled the crate into the far back of the car. "Someone fucked up big." My dad didn't disagree and when the guy asked, "How much it weigh?" my dad said, "Didn't weigh it. A hundred twenty-five, maybe. Dressed out."

"Damn shame," the guy said, but softly this time, as if to himself, and there followed no small talk about trichinosis or insurance claims or evening any score. My dad said thanks for the assistance, and before we pulled away the guy lowered his head by my window, and when I rolled it down he patted my elbow and said, "Drive easy," though I was in the passenger's seat, at least to start out. "It's murder this time of day on the interstate," he said. "Crazies everywhere."

But I felt safe once we started for home, and after only a few miles we switched off, me driving while my dad closed his eyes for long stretches, the heater on the lowest setting and his forehead pressed against the cold glass. We talked hardly at all, and I wondered if I should pull over and get out and pack the crate with snow once we got far enough north.

But except for gas and pee stops we pushed straight through, and once it got dark my dad stayed behind the wheel, and not intending to I nonetheless dozed off. We'd never lived on a farm, but that's what I was dreaming. A barn full of slaughtered hogs hanging upside down from the crossbeams. Front legs cut off at the elbows, and my dad holding not a knife but a cane cutter, and the steamy, scalded insides of the carcasses rising a vaporous pale pink all the way up into the rafters.

Maybe I started to scream—I don't know—but my dad, he kept shaking my shoulder and saying, "Sy. Hey, you all right?" and when we swung onto County Line a few minutes later I guess I was, though it took the blue light from a TV blinking in the window of a trailer house I recognized to erase that other image. I'd driven over this way in better weather with Billy Pipes, who named this exact same unpaved dead end Lover's Lane. The perfect place, he said, to sweet talk Megan Sacksteder or Jeannine Capinski into saving our souls. But here I was instead with my dad, the ass end of the station wagon sliding back and forth as he powered all the way up to the top of the hill, snow clots slapping hard in the wheel wells.

He stopped and angled the car so that the low beams floated a few feet above the snow on the downslope to the river, a kind of chute banked on all sides by the darkness. I couldn't hear the water, not even after we got out and dragged the crate to where we could see better, and for a few minutes we stood there until he started to shiver. I should have thought to bring him a coat, and I said so, and he answered back, "Get the tire iron, Sy." And when he pried open the top slats they snapped in the cold like rifle fire. I half turned away but the smell wasn't all that terrible, and the moon was out now, too, a perfect crescent. Like a single tusk, I almost said, but thought better of it. Orion, the hunter, was up there somewhere, the entire sky suddenly alive with aligning planets and stars.

"Give me a hand here," my dad said, and he was shaking like he'd been sitting too long in a deer blind, the wind kicking up but still enough light to see by.

"Ready?" he said, and I mouthed the numbers as he counted, and, on three, we heaved together. The boar spilled out all soft and loose jointed onto the frozen ground. I noticed that its eyes were open and glassy and reflecting the moonlight. I had on the only pair of gloves, and when I bent down and grabbed one rear leg, my dad grabbed the other. The double effort made for easy sliding, and as soon as I felt the heavy tug on the downward pitch, I let go. But my dad? He sat back hard on his haunches, his boot heels digging in like he was locked in a tug of war, the weight and strain of a once-in-a lifetime all but faded away. A sweet run of luck gone bad and *Hey, if that's all you're holding?* And so I watched as the boar's impossible bulk hugged the hard crust, the dips and rises and just one time spinning backward as if to finally glimpse us beyond the tips of those gleaming white razors.

The Farmers Almanac, they're predicting the worst winter in decades. That's what my dad had said at suppertime the night before he left. He'd talked winterkill and how 'bout I muzzle load with him after he got back? Winterkill, I thought, and under the avalanche of snows yet to come, the only wild boar in the state would freeze and thaw a second time and begin to decompose for good in the Michigan spring. And the advent of warmer days come April and May so welcome to those of us who hunkered down and somehow survived the season, unable to get away.

[Sky Riders]

IN LATE AUGUST, our dads off on their National Guard duty, me and Iwo patrolled the town's outskirts on our motorbikes, the Aurora Borealis igniting the entire sky like tracer fire. Like *incoming*, we'd yell, and balls-to-brains we'd bend low over our handlebars and retreat full throttle down the dust-rutted two-track under the power lines.

Hot Rain, Lady Luck, Sweet Rot we named our operations as we convoyed across the weedy-green streambed, our knobby rear tires rocketing the water scum skyward. And while our dads wheezed themselves into shape with two weeks of pushups and squat thrusts on the drill fields of Camp Grayling, we raided their cigarettes and Canadian Club, our hair close-cropped and the camouflaged sleeves of our T-shirts rolled tight.

And, seized from the depths of Mr. Jakiella's low bureau bottom drawer, a condom apiece. Our first rubbers ever, ribbed and lubricated Trojans, which we flipped in our palms like weightless square quarters. Flipped and flipped them as if that might forestall the departure of Stephanie Dilligaff to somewhere called Winnipeg. In her image we'd discovered beauty supreme, beauty unflawed by the fury of our adoration, so absolute it might have burdened the bearer had she so much as paused to acknowledge us. Had she, we would gladly—each of us in turn—have taken a bullet for her. Let Stephanie D. enter my line of sight, and previously undiscovered places inside me trembled and ached.

Iwo's all-time favorite flick was *Planet of the Apes*, and hammer-browed under his helmet he reminded me of fierce General Ursus, a soldier's soldier riding headlong into the dark-scarlet eye of the cauldron. We suppressed admitting that our Guardsmen dads, reservists who'd signed on for the paycheck and nothing else, bore no resemblance to that or any other kind of fire.

Company Diggity is what we dubbed ourselves, after some goof tune from the fifties that Iwo liked and sang, sometimes all the way back to base camp, where my mom kept the porch light burning. And where we slap-fought each other black and blue in my backyard, those lyrics rising through the thin glow of that single halogen mounted on a pole outside my dad's upholstery shop: *Hot diggity, dog ziggity, boom what you do to me*. Lyrics as dumb as garden grubs, but that's how we trained in the summer of 1989, the year Iwo Jakiella and I turned fourteen.

AWOL is how my mom saw my dad's departure. Not unlike his disappearances to Little Orphan Annie's, the all-night bar a few klicks outside Mancelona on old Route 41, from which he retreated to sleep in his upholstery shop, a converted four-car garage, where he stacked the skeletons of couches like abandoned barrack bunks. No sign out front, and no regular hours. Just a white cardboard clock with movable red hands indicating what time he'd be in, and maybe even would be, but too angry or ashamed or too hung over to answer if I knocked.

"Dad?" I'd say. "Are you in there? Answer me if you are, okay? Please?"

He never would, but then, in the silence of the house, I'd hear again, some sleepless late night, those muffled love moans wending up through the heat register from the downstairs bedroom. Another long-awaited cease-fire, I imagined, in the household wars that had raged off and on for as long as I could remember.

My dad's name, Blaze Krug, is my legal name too, though from day one everybody always called me Buzz. Like Iwo, I was an only child. Unless, of course, you factored our status as blood brothers, each summer lancing and pressing the dark pulp of our thumbs together until they stuck.

Iwo was part Pottawattamie, on his mom's side. A dark-skinned skinny-minnie with antelope legs and one of those built-up black shoes on his right foot. Every other step he took ended with a lethal leg-whip, plus that unmistakable pelvic hitch in his gait. Like something weight-bearing in perpetual collapse but never giving way or for one second slowing him down.

The industrial waste pits—that was my mom's take on Iwo's birth defect, given the trailer park's proximity to the recently shutdown gypsum plant where Iwo's dad had served as a foreman for twenty-two years before the layoffs turned him inward and moody. He attempted to mop up in the aftermath, his unemployment benefits all but zapped, but by all accounts the prospects going forward were pretty scant. On certain moonlit nights, from atop Bald Hill, you could see, rising from deep down in the hardpan all around there, a luminous, greenish glow cast helter-skelter, as if from countless mangled highway spacers.

"Their choice to ride out the risks," my dad insisted, whenever my mom would broach the subject. "You pull a living wage in bad times, but it's an odds player's bet." Then he'd boast that same rag about having done his share of gambling, one time with other people's money—a more than moderate stake he'd lifted from the till where he used to tend bar some weekend nights at an off-ramp Ramada somewhere downstate. Kalamazoo or Cadillac. Had he lost, "Well, we're probably talking hard time, Buzz. The law gets involved, you better shit-can all claims on any promissory note you wrote yourself. But hey, sometimes circumstances dictate and you got no other play but to roll the damn dice. Go ahead," he'd always say, as if reaching the sole reason for the retelling. "Ask your mother if that ain't the way *most* things in this life shake out."

The one and only time I turned to her for corroboration on this she said, "I never lived in a turtleback. At least not in any of *those* I didn't." Meaning the decrepit company mobiles, that tight cloverleaf of them with their dinky lots and mismatched storage sheds, a sizable number of them already padlocked and condemned, the windows either boarded or peppered with BB holes, and with weeds growing right through the floors. Some of the loudmouths at school referred to the dwellings as misery tins and, cheap talk notwithstanding, it wasn't a designation anyone still residing there needed to be reminded of. Whenever I was within earshot, I'd tell those clucks to go piss up a rope. I'd walk straight toward them, no matter how outnumbered I was, and I'd say it point-blank to their faces. As in, "Bring it on, you derringer dicks," as they backpedaled away from the wrath of my stare-down and my already coiled fists.

Our house was a good mile distant from the trailer park, a shutterless white two-story with dormer windows, a full basement, and a roof pitched low against the harsher elements: snow that never seemed to stop and those killer arctic blasts that all but buried us for months in darkness. Plus a satellite dish in the backyard big enough, as Iwo used to joke, to pick up heartbeats on Mars. A palace compared to Iwo's place, and set back off the road on a high elevation no less, and if common sense—as my dad maintained—dictated that toxins leached downhill, away from us, then I'd simply blame a vile God for denying my mom more kids.

It wasn't a secret that she'd wanted a large family, and badly, and it was my dad's poor choice of words that kicked off the trouble one morning when he said that if she didn't slow down trying *he'd* be disfigured for good. No doubt he intended it only to be funny. Even flirty was a possible interpretation, but I couldn't comprehend it as such. More to the point, I hated how he nose-chortled and winked over at me before sliding his chair back from the breakfast table as she retreated into the bathroom. Where I imagined her thumb-rubbing her temples and staring transfixed into the emptiness of the mirror, her skin glowing ghost white, even in late summer. She always wore her hair chopped short and shaped like a pulled-back funeral veil. As black as winter ash, I thought, matching perfectly those pouchy half circles under her dark, deep-set, slightly oversized gray eyes.

It wasn't her normal habit to both shut *and* lock the door, but on that particular occasion she did. And stayed in there a long while, my dad leaning back on the chair's hind legs, and his eyes burning hard in her direction.

"Buzz," he said, "when it comes to the opposite sex, take it from someone who's been there and survived to tell the tale—women don't fight fair. As God is my witness, they don't. No way, no how. Period." He said no man ever lived or ever would who was gifted enough with love to sustain it long-term the way most women needed but never got.

"How come?" I asked. "Why's that?" And he said, "Biological deficiency," to which, according to him, the species had forever been held hostage, "Right up until and including this very day. And, in all likelihood, every other day hereafter." He said that short of some divine intervention we were destined to repeat the calamities of women and men. "Can't be helped," he said. "It's all there in black and white, Buzz. Right there in the Old Testament. Read it and weep."

Maybe so, I thought, but Iwo and me? Uh-uh. We'd confab tirelessly about tracing with our fingertips the entire inseam of some girl's skintight Levi's. Sooner or later it was bound to happen. And possibly, rewarded for our vigilance and valor, we'd even get to unzip those blue jeans and finger-fumble our way smack-dab into the sweet, dark heat of her curlies, though back then neither of us had ever gotten close, the Casanovas of absolutely nobody's secret whims and tingles.

Not so much as a kiss or caress or a single flirtatious word whispered. Didn't matter. The prospect alone validated our futures, and that very night after the Dilligaffs moved away, we performed synchronized side-by-side wheelies down the entire length of Stephanie D's block. Her house was pitch dark, and the gasoline-nitro concoction we'd mixed and poured into our tanks ignited for a few lingering seconds the charred pavement below our tailpipes: brilliant orange-and-blue wavering fire-tails, as if a comet had skidded through the neighborhood, the thin aftermath of smoke rising beyond the rooftops.

That summer during the two weeks when our dads were away, Iwo lived at our house, given his mom's sudden departure not quite a year before and her exact whereabouts still unknown. "Gypsy genes," was how my dad explained her disappearance, though no single, immediate, actual cause could be attributed. For sure not by him, and if Iwo had a clue he wasn't saying. Not outright anyway, as if taking sides against either parent fingered him as the betrayer of any legitimate hope for reconciliation on the home front.

The closest he came to blaming anyone occurred that afternoon we discovered and hauled out of the mobile a fat stack of *Playboys*. Fully exposed centerfolds who smiled up at us as we force-fed them one by one into the flames of a fifty-gallon drum that roared and roared like the voice of hellfire itself.

"Bullshit by the bucket, Buzz, that's all it is," he said, and for a panicked few seconds I figured—when he turned and headed back inside—that he had in mind to torch the place, his dad's initialed, brushed-chrome Zippo still in hand. Had he appealed to me to help him, I'm uncertain even now what I might have done or said.

We had the key to Iwo's house trailer and orders to recon every couple of days, a quick sweep just to check things out. Maybe heat up a can of Chef Boyardee spaghetti and meatballs if we got hungry. "Just remember to turn off the stove is all. And listen up. No wild parties or loose girls in here," Mr. Jakiella had emphatically warned, his throat razor burned. A single, tiny wad of Kleenex bloomed red as a poppy on his Adam's apple every time it bobbed high up on his neck, while he fixed on each of us with that hard to read, deep-eyed glare he'd started to use more and more. First on Iwo and then on me. One to the other and back again as we both stood at attention, slowly nodding, and flabbergasted that he'd actually conceived of us carrying on in such a manner behind his back.

"Yes, sir," we assured him in unison. Loud and clear, while our insubordinate hearts cried out in our chests that *not* dying virgins preempted every other potential consideration, and that included orders from our own dads if need be.

That single devotion above all else. And yet now those no-name, glossy-colored nudes had set Iwo off big-time ballistic. Like I'd never witnessed before, which made no sense, given the number of times we'd sneak-previewed magazines like *Hustler* and *Penthouse*. But somehow that day, the collective weight of all those naked paper bodies morphed in Iwo's mind into one colossal, fire-breathing, hydra-headed whore.

Which is the term he used when he finally reemerged, squinty-eyed like maybe he'd been crying, a lit Lucky Strike between his lips. "Flippin' whores," he said, inhaling deeply and holding the smoke in his lungs for a long time before blowing it out. This was the same Iwo who, for the sake of morale, had smuggled a pinup into our original hideout underneath the company loading dock, where all our top-secret, highest priority command-center briefings took place. She was a brunette in high heels and with a bikini line so luminous as to magnify even further the mystery residing in that tapered V between her thighs. And those nipples we swore to each other we could detonate with the tips of our tongues.

Iwo had momentarily snapped was all, uncovering that cache of contraband under his own parents' bed. Not exactly standard operating procedure, even for a dad with a wife missing in action, given that he also had a teenage son who hadn't heard word one from her in months. Not so much as a postcard or phone call.

But, "Come on," I wanted to say. "So it ain't Merry Christmas in July, okay? So what? There's lots worse things a kid could stumble on." Though I guess to Iwo's way of thinking his dad might just as well have been shagging a piece of strange right there in front of us, the entire trailer rocking like a boat.

Occasionally it did just that during turbid wind-spews or storms. And now in the distance we could hear thunder-boomers and see above

us the swollen blue veins of the sky darkening fast, the clouds hump-
backed and beginning to roll. Like a major downpour was headed our
way, the shotgun dwellings in that silvery-gray light turning even ti-
nier. And Iwo standing on the top cinder block of the makeshift stairs,
railing big time as I flashed on who or what the two of *us* might be
like in another twenty-five years—married and in love with girls we
had yet to meet, but nevertheless already beset, like our parents, by
that same perpetual bicker and heartbreak that *their* lives had somehow become? In a single blindsided blink, Iwo and I turned old and
overweight and were drinking forty-ouncers in front of the TV, while
blustering on half-cocked about the mercenary ways of the world.

Talk about ass-backward and surreal. Wrong reading was all, or
so I told myself, just a cockeyed brain blip, nothing more. Still, it sure
creeped me out—that premonition of us as knockoffs of the dads we'd
long ago taken up arms against, chanting our motto like an anthem:
"Yield to nothing, surrender to no one." We were, after all, young and
vehement and in control, and so we vowed to each other, over and
over, that we'd never—not in this or in a thousand other lifetimes—
foul up that badly as husbands and fathers no matter where or how we
ended up serving in this world.

I mentioned none of this to Iwo. Instead I said, "Hey, time to rock
and roll," and when I pointed up as if the whole sky might heave loose,
he turned and snap-flicked his cigarette hard against the front door,
sparks ricocheting in a halo around him. "My mom," I said. "Come on,
we gotta highball it." But he stayed facing away, as if wherever *he'd*
shambled off to in his head was a place he couldn't quite navigate back
from, suddenly all jelly-kneed and flat out of breath.

It was an eerie-weird Iwo moment, though he seemed okay again as
we tore-ass across the Malicks' back eighty, right between the waist-
high cornrows and up past the crib barn to the access road that intersected the towering high-tension lines. From there we had just a
quick-hitch sprint to our promontory outpost that overlooked Route
664, where we'd hit our kill switches and wait for my mom, rain or
shine.

No binoculars, but sometimes I'd circle each eye with my forefinger and thumb, pretending to glass the far hills, the valley bottomlit with goldenrod and Queen Anne's lace, and my mom's cherry-red four-barrel Chevy Impala as conspicuous as a trip-flare, the road that time of day otherwise deserted. She never once forgot to slow down on that low crest beyond the shelter-belt of sycamores, where she'd lean forward and watch for us up there, straddling our motorbikes and flailing our arms. If she double-tooted, it meant a double shift and that me and Iwo would either have to motor down to Dingman's, where she worked as a waitress serving chuck steaks and navy beans, or commandeer dinner on our own.

A single toot was our code for an early, post–happy hour knockoff. Nineteen hundred hours, give or take. Which I much preferred so she wouldn't have to walk out alone to her car in the dark, her uniform skimpy and scoop-necked, tempting some local just lonely or messed up enough to fantasize getting his ticket punched right there in the parking lot. "For gracious sakes," my mom, all tired smiles, would say, whenever we'd be waiting there to escort her home. A single-car cavalcade, like she was some dignitary, eyeliner and lipstick and matching red nails, her Impala flanked by two dirt-caked metallic-black Phantom scramblers. Iwo and I would break formation after a half mile or so, downshifting and veering off-road across ditch lines and fields and gullies, spumes of vapor-fire from the natural gas wells shooting heavenward.

Some nights it was so bright I'd turn off my headlight, the giant sprocket of the stars seeming to tumble toward me no matter which way I looped or leaned, the nocturnal world in a perpetual slow-motion freefall that never actually fell. Like a certain recurring dream I used to have of leaping over buses and railroad cars, suspended above the town like E.T., minus that goofy, single-speed bicycle with the basket and bell on the handlebars. A diehard sky rider silhouetted against the full moon. That's how I once described it to Iwo.

"Yeah, a sky rider," he fired back. "That's called a *wet* dream, Buzz. You checked your bottom sheet lately?"—and the way we howled at that was downright *dog ziggity*, the tune alive again on his lips as we juked and jabbed in the thin ghost-light outside my dad's shop. And zigzagging all around us those bats we believed we might have snagged from the air had we reached straight up and squeezed our sweaty, open palms into knuckles and fists.

Fourteen and lovesick and officially left in charge. No wonder we war-whooped that fatal afternoon and ransacked whatever we could that might rid our world of boredom, attacked it like storm troopers, the adrenaline pump primed with the prospect of additional contraband. More unfiltered cigarettes and booze, and what we believed were blasting caps, pilfered from one of the company sheds, though tossed grenade-style from our knees onto the burn barrel's red-hot cinders they turned out duds, every last one. And our dads' firearms oiled and trigger-locked and stored—along with buck knives and boxes of ammo and leather cartridge belts—in the dark, airtight, fireproof bellies of their gun safes.

Our entire arsenal consisted of Iwo's pellet rifle, and the plan was to pump it and pump it until the pressure of a single shot penetrating a can of Mr. Jakiella's Burma-Shave would turn the undersides of the oak leaves in his backyard a gooey, glistening, sticky-dripping viscous white. The consistency of egg whites, or the gelatinous goop surrounding sinew and bones that made up the human body, we imagined.

Iwo was already in prone position, legs splayed out, right eye to the peep sight, and I was about to place the shaken pressurized shaving cream can on that lowest limb, when we both glanced back toward his house—and there was Iwo's mom. At first she said nothing. Not even after she slid her sunglasses up top of her forehead, her face flushed and her cobalt-colored eyes wide and bead-hard on Iwo in a way I'd never seen eyes take aim at another person before.

The afternoon was high humidity, mid-ninety degrees outside. That brutal choke-hold kind of swelter that whomped down on us so that even shirtless in the heavy shade, we endured the slow bake of blisters on our necks and shoulder blades, our bodies sweating bullets no matter how slowly we'd clean-sneak toward any unsuspecting enemy target.

But Mrs. Jakiella—she redefined hot and miserable, the insufferable dog days having taken a terrible toll on her. Like she'd just escaped from a pit oven or from some cannibal's cook pot, her thin white sundress soaked and clinging so tightly to her flesh that I could see the indentation of her belly button showing through, and the not so vague shadow of her underthings. Nobody spoke. The only sound was the explosive *crackle-hiss* of cicadas surging alive, the air electric with them, and from the looks of this woman I could surmise only that she must have trudged from a considerable distance in order to arrive here in that condition. Maybe from as far away as Nine Mile, where a person figuring to stash a rust-riddled Vega for a while might do just that, undetected, behind the railroad spur. But if so, if that *had* been her strategy, then why in creation's name would she have worn those open-toed dress shoes hardly designed for foot travel over loose gravel and dirt?

Shell-shocked seemed the only viable theory. Worn and war-weary. And had I a single wish to call in right then it would have been to vanish, literally, as in *poof*—any and all trace of me instantaneously erased from the force field of Mrs. Jakiella's consciousness. Though truth be told, she never even gave a look in my direction and no doubt wasn't addressing me in the least when she finally cleared her throat and said, barely above a whisper, "Come inside. Please," her voice cracking on just those three words.

It took a full fifteen or twenty stunned seconds for us to reestablish our bearings. And to shoot each other a high alert before following her into the trailer, the screen door spring-loaded and slapping shut behind us, stopping us in our tracks. We both hung back at that point, stock-still and speechless and watching her every move as she crossed into the kitchen and without hesitation twisted on the cold water tap—I assumed to refill the ice cube tray that we'd left out, but she never touched it. Nor the pint of Canadian Club, which I quickly calculated from where I was positioned closest to the door measured approximately one-half depleted.

"On the rocks. How else?" I'd quipped the previous evening, and, after Iwo had slow-nodded and poured, we high-fived a bunch of times, all cocky-like and smirking at the good fortune of our spoils. Smirked and clinked glasses as Iwo said back, "That'd be us all right," as if, armed with a drink and a smoke and a temporary pad all our own, we'd risen perhaps not in rank but unmistakably in stature. After a silent ten-count to bask in that glory, I said, "Cheers."

"Yep, to you and me, Mr. Buzz Krug. Bottoms up," Iwo said, and in unison we did, our throats scorched instantly raw, and the two of us cursing and coughing and stomping in wild, madmen circles, as if attempting to put out a brush fire barefoot.

Still, I liked the free-floating sensation that ensued, the trailer in a slow, easy sway. And how those first few stars outside the kitchen window appeared impossibly close by, as if maybe the trailer wasn't a boat after all, but rather the Starship *Enterprise*, and we, the peace-keepers of the galaxies, were out there doing our finest, most noteworthy, semi-inebriated Vulcan impersonations.

But now, sober and earth-grounded, I was focused, and focused *only* on how Mrs. Jakiella's dress hem rode up past the backs of her bare knees. And, pitched forward like she was, how her calves took hard shape in the lift of those shoes, the heels all scuffed and crudded up and a silver bangle on her right ankle that I'd only previously seen teenage girls—the heartthrob likes of Stephanie D. and Sylvia Wein-traub—wear.

Had we reconnoitered at my house instead of at the trailer, my mom, before leaving for work, would have replenished the lemonade and iced tea in the refrigerator and, as always, stockpiled a couple cans of Hires root beer or Fanta grape. Something cold we could have offered Mrs. Jakiella, maybe to mix with some bourbon if she wanted, the way I'd seen her drink it on occasion well before midday to help calm her nerves. But at our immediate disposal was nothing other than that potentially contaminated lukewarm water, and I hadn't a clue how long she intended to waggle her spread fingers under the open tap. Or why. Or what unfathomable, convoluted line of thinking must have been taking place inside her mind after so much time away.

Outwardly at least, Mrs. Jakiella resembled her former self. Slim hips and shoulders like a girl, and if you blurred your vision it wasn't that far-fetched to eradicate a bunch of years from her face. From my vantage, not the slightest sign of her backside in sag or early collapse like those of most other moms her age. No gray hair or varicose veins, either. None that I could see, anyway, and I had no trouble whatsoever imagining how she might arouse in certain men any number of lost or dying passions. Yet all the while she was looking more and more, with every passing second, like a woman who didn't feel young or pretty, and who didn't intend to stay around very long, that option possibly no longer available to her anyhow.

I'd always liked Mrs. Jakiella, a baleful, soft-spoken lady who used to sub at the junior high. Our district being underfunded and sometimes short-handed, they'd hire not out-of-work teachers but available local moms. Science, Spanish, remedial English—didn't matter the subject or grade level, and it wasn't at all unusual, for an entire class period, for Mrs. Jakiella to switch off the lights and draw those heavy gray-green canvas window shades tight to the sills. Like instant nightfall, at which point she'd hold up her glow-in-the-dark star charts, naming and identifying for us the various constellations. "Cassiopeia," she'd say, "and there's Andromeda and Perseus." And she'd explain how they, among others not yet seen or named, formed the Milky Way. It always took a few minutes for my vision to adjust enough to make out the contours of her face: angled cheekbones, that slight tilt of her jaw, and her eyes oddly illumined as if they, too, were part of the celestial display. What I noticed most and never tired of was the way she'd smile whenever she described Orion and his dogs, and how they hunted all night above the hills and fields and the woodlots directly above our houses while we slept.

Same day and place a single summer past, and Mrs. Jakiella might have been washing and peeling potatoes without me even noticing. Just my best buddy's mom at the sink. But as soon as she started to shoulder-shake there was no mistaking that everything in our brief lives had already and forever been unalterably changed, and that a full-spill gusher was on the way. Painful, deep-squelching intakes of breath as if in this swelter she'd started to shiver or hyperventilate, followed by low guttural moans and sobs the likes of which I'd never encountered and reasoned that only a person acknowledging a ruined life could make.

Iwo did not say, "Mom?" and he did not go to her. When she turned to face us, her lips were so tightly torqued I believed she might, right there in front us, begin to consume entire parts of herself. And me, gawking at her in the smolder of that cramped, low-ceilinged room, absent a single fan or the slightest cross breeze. I could barely breathe—my throat closing up and the air heavy and stifling as if long trapped in a tunnel or a sealed-up underground backyard bomb shelter.

The wall clock's second hand seemed to click half-speed, and it came to me that if we remained there for even a minute longer, our fate would be to suffocate, gagging on whatever last-gasp effort we might attempt to justify any arrangement of who or what we were and believed.

That's when I wheeled and fled outside to my motorbike, uttering not a sound, and never once slowing down or glancing back.

Not then and not now, but certain nights in dreams, I still hear those intermittent thuds of Iwo's right foot, like a distant drum on the linoleum floor. Blue and warped and worn dull as sea glass where his mom stood bawling that day by the kitchen sink with the water running.

And me downshifting and throttling hard in full retreat to get back home as fast as I could. Safe and alone, and out of the heat.

Keeper of my dad's shop key in his absence, my mom saw no reason to hide or secure it. Or to wear it around her neck like a medal. Like the dog tags he'd slip off after his two simulated weeks at war, when he became, once again, a normal civilian dad and husband and self-employed upholsterer, reputedly the finest around. If, of course, you could only pin him down.

So, on that August afternoon when I arrived home from Iwo's, my mom still at work, the key was in plain view on the kitchen table. Although the shop was off-limits to me, I unlocked the door and switched on the air conditioner. An oversized window unit that if you cranked to highest power and stood directly in its cold, undulant current for a stationary ten minutes, you could see the smoky blue vapor of your breath. "Better than a backyard swimming pool," as my dad said after the installation, the two of us standing side by side, laughing and pointing at the goose bumps forming on each other's forearms, the tips of our eyelashes turning white.

First it was naps and then all-nighters that he took on that same sleeper sofa where I laid down, lights off, and closed my eyes. Listening to those first few plunking drops of rain on the aluminum roof, I dreamed of him in his combat fatigues, squinty-eyed and drawing down on a silhouette field target of a young boy. A life-sized training exercise replica, possibly booby-trapped, possibly not. "How long before a family-man infantry soldier clicks off the safety and squeezes the trigger? Imagine," he said in a stuttering voice I hardly recognized. "Just imagine if you were wrong."

I had no idea how long I'd slept when I heard my mom say, "Hey?" her voice sounding far off, as if, like Mrs. Jakiella, *she'd* been away a long time, too. "Buzz," she said, "you're shaking, sweetheart." And, when I fully awakened, damp and disoriented and freezing cold, there she was, sitting right next to me and rubbing my neck and back to warm me up.

"Where's Iwo?" she said. "I didn't see his motorbike, and he's not in your bedroom. Is everything okay? Are the two of you all right? Buzz, look at me."

I rolled over onto my back and folded my arms across my chest, the uneven heave of my ribcage rising and falling, and my heart, caved in somewhere inside there, thrumming and thrumming in my forehead and ears. "You're not sick or hurt, are you?" she asked, and pressed the back of her hand to my forehead, as if checking to see if I had a fever. I could barely make out her face, maybe an impossible foot away was all, and when she bent down to kiss me I started to cry.

"What's wrong?" she said. "Whatever it is, just tell me. Tell me right now, okay?" And after a few minutes I did, answering whatever questions I could. No, just her, just Mrs. Jakiella, nobody else, and I didn't think so but yes, it was possible, I supposed, that she'd been dropped off by somebody. My mom's mind, I could tell, was spinning double and triple time to piece the fragments together.

"Show me," she said, "take me there." Code for *I want you close to me*, and so I followed her into the house, where she didn't even change out of her waitress uniform, other than to slip on her flip-flops after phoning the Jakiellas' trailer, and then leaving a note for Iwo on our kitchen table. "In case he shows up back here while we're gone," she said.

I knew he wouldn't. But I switched on the porch light, exactly as my mom always did—until, as she put it, we were safely tucked in. Me in my bed and Iwo on the air mattress beside me on the floor, where we'd debrief while our eyes adjusted to the dark, the room slowly dilating and reforming itself around us in muted shades of black and white.

It hadn't rained much, or cooled down beyond a few degrees, the roads dry as desert bones and the moon's intermittent luster silvery on the treetops. Like that first hard frost when I'd help my dad haul out the ladders and double hang the windows to hold back the onslaught of the impending winter's wrath.

Held hostage by the seasons. That's what my mom in her moods sometimes said, and I said it too, mostly to Iwo, who concurred that only losers would live a lifetime in a place so bottomed out. So nowhere, as he used to say every morning right before we kick-started our motorbikes and headed out to invade the new day's original light.

There were lamps burning in maybe half a dozen of the mobiles. Low-wattage and filmy yellow, and I didn't see a single person inside as we passed. My mom pulled into the Jakiellas' driveway, a mere parking strip of cracked concrete and weeds, where she shifted into park but left the engine running. The windows were down, and I could hear a dog barking. My mom was fully concentrating and staring straight ahead, like maybe she expected Iwo and his mom to step out and wave, the way they used to whenever I'd be dropped off there for the day. That same routine played out for years before we traded up from banana-seat bikes to the real thing.

Like mine, my mom's hands were long fingered. She was squeezing the steering wheel, her face flat-hued and scared, and I flashed on Iwo and his mom somewhere miles distant from where we were parked. I searched in vain for any sign of them, or of anything we might use to trace back through the events that had become this night in our lives.

"Mom, there's nobody here," I said. "They're gone already." She nodded but exited the car anyway and knocked on the Jakiellas' front door a couple of times, and then reaching left she tapped with her fingernails on the dark pane. Why, I didn't know, but when she turned back around into the headlights, her eyes shone like red-hot iron filings. Like a surprise flash snapshot taken at night. A woman in an off-white waitress uniform, alone and hugging her shoulders outside a half-dilapidated and abandoned trailer.

That image. As if the blame for all that had happened was somehow hers and hers alone.

I think more often now about how recklessly love misfires, making traitors of us all. Had my dad not imbibed and caroused and suffered my mom's three miscarriages with bouts of increased rancor and grief, he would have had no need or reason to enlist in the service of Uncle

Sam. And yet he continued out of habit long after an unexpected calm had settled around us, making us feel like a family again. Quiet talk at the table, and my dad less inclined to drink like he did, nightly and in excess. I submit that I have since experimented with everything from therapy to hypnosis, including alcohol, but that I cannot, even as a vaguest glimmer, recollect any of my mom's pregnancies, which has led me to believe that I was never told.

And that each must have ended early term, before names were bandied about, and well before she began to show. And that the final moratorium on my parents' trying just one last time did not signal the defeat of their marriage, but rather served oddly to quell the deep-seated fear that each conception must have wrought in each of them. I'd been spared the details but have since had them clarified during certain halting conversations with my mom.

Conversations mostly about my dad, who claimed he could hem or slipcover a dogwood or willow. Or sheathe the disappearing half moon in a raiment of gold. He, Blaze Krug, who died not in a foreign war but during live ordinance maneuvers on the base. We buried him on a day when the air had that slightly sulfurous odor that was always present after a rain. A small funeral, absent of any military presence, save the obligatory tri-fold flag.

I am thirty-four years old as of last October, and crazy in love with a woman who handcrafts brass sundials in a studio attached to the house in which we live. She likes visiting my mom, who always serves us tea or coffee and who just last week, right out of the blue, asked if I ever heard from Iwo.

"No, never," I said. "Not in over a decade."

I told her I doubted that I would, and got up from my chair, and walked to the window, evening already coming on. I don't know why, but when I squeezed shut my eyes, there we were. The two of us rising up again on the foot pegs of our motorbikes as we hurtled homeward side by side over every next lip and rise, that last light of day dying out behind us on some impossibly faraway fiery-red skyline.

[The World of a Few Minutes Ago]

after a line by Gregory Djanikian

MY NAME IS CLYDE FRYSINGER and my wife, Mary-Helen, is asleep upstairs in the spare bedroom down the hall. A recent and unexpected move, for which no explanation has been offered, and I haven't, nor will I, inquire as to why. We are—the two of us—and for a long time now, childless, and separated in age by only a few months, and suddenly pushing deep into our seventies. After fifty-three years of marriage, our days only vaguely intersect, and maybe *this* is the reason I am still awake and standing in the backyard, the stars at predictable intervals exploding across the sky.

Were she to look down she might mistake me for that prowler she insisted used to visit during my extended absences before I retired, though as far as I know there has never been a single confirmed sighting reported elsewhere in this neighborhood of vintage Victorian homes. No sudden run on deadbolts and not a single vigilante crime fighter rallying the troops for a community watch. And for sure no intermittent crisscross of searchlights sweeping the premises, though

I have spent much of my life in places steeped deep in the madness of human misery and violence. As Buffalo Bill Cody put it: "If there is no God, then I am his prophet." I say, amen for owning up.

"Clyde, please. Don't go." Mary-Helen's anthem, and rubbing her temples, she'd say, "Not so soon." But there I'd be, boarding a plane again, and putting down so far distant of dreamland I'd sometimes forget where I was from. A lifelong Wolverine, born and raised, my son's bedroom, now the spare room where Mary-Helen sleeps, still decorated in blue and maize. I might even have cast back on that while camped outside the compound of the Branch Davidians in Waco, Texas, April 1993, nineteenth day of the month. On assignment, where late morning I photographed hellfire so fierce I had to duck and quick-pivot away. And on the blind run shoot backward, over my shoulder, camera aimed into the roar of flames that consumed, nationwide, the covers of magazines such as *Newsweek* and *Time* and *U.S. News & World Report*.

Whenever I returned from assignment, Mary-Helen's insistence that she had seen the prowler was a barometer of my extended absence. "He's real. He's there outside the house in plain view. Sometimes he looks right at me," she would say, almost in a whisper, and certain nights to calm her down I would sit at the window seat waiting in darkness for him to arrive—figment or phantom or Peeping Tom. "Other times he's merely a glimpse in the occluded moonlight. Here and gone, Clyde. Silent and ghostlike." And later, while undressing for bed, I would not only imagine him out there, but imagine that I *was* him. This presence occupied my thoughts in a way that I now understand is characteristic of men who have been betrayed by great loss and hopelessness and by the desperate and simultaneous onset of wild and unrestrained desire.

The patio is directly to my left and illuminated by the full moon's blue penumbra. Perhaps I will make my slow way over there to finish this nightcap of bourbon I am holding, and stare out toward the garden where just this morning Mary-Helen pruned her lush and carefully tended hybrid roses, the fresh-cut redolence of them already long vanished. Right now, nothing seems so improbable as the world of a few minutes ago.

Remember Sergeant Joe Friday? "The facts ma'am, only the facts." Here's one: I am no stranger to sin, no model of moral reckoning. As a former AP photographer I am still prone to night terrors and torrential sweats seconds before the onset of first light. I come wide-awake, imagining my right eye pressed to the viewfinder, my night-vision camera turning the surrounding darkness an eerie green. I think of war that way, by the colors mostly, and by the chemical smells. Vietnam first. Later Nicaragua, and, tending toward the end of my career, Bosnia and Rwanda. One evening, a flak jacket saved my life, but I have never once strapped on a sidearm or carried a weapon of any kind for self-defense. Had I been drafted I would have fled this country in a heartbeat.

Domestically I have covered a dozen executions, men and women both, at least two of the condemned wrongly convicted, as we now know, the death chambers as stark and blighted and bright white as butcher paper. Conrad had it right: the horror, the horror, and in the aftermath of mass suicides I have tiptoed among the corpses. I was there at Jonestown. Hale-Bopp is a late credit of mine, shot *not* in the comet's tail but rather in a nondescript house packed with bunk beds, the bodies neatly laid out, each face covered by a shroud of purple cloth. Black shirts and sweatpants, identical black Nikes. I touched nothing. I later read that seven of these men had voluntarily been castrated somewhere in Mexico. They wore triangular patches that said "Heaven's Gate Away Team," and died with a five-dollar bill and three shiny quarters in their pockets. Vodka and phenobarbital. It's true— too much of anything will kill you dead. I repeat: it will kill you dead.

It is likely that you have seen me during TV news clips over the years, that guy in the background on one knee, leaning in, focusing? Yes, that is me, the same figure who, when he moves, moves slowly and says nothing, but refuses to turn away. Maybe it's for the sake of the paycheck or the coverage itself, the need to expose, but either way, as Jesus is my witness, I manipulate not a single detail of what I've recorded.

Fact: in Mary-Helen's mind there is no difference between the downy breast feathers of songbirds that visit our feeders and those dried rose petals that occasionally spiral down from the inside covers of our books.

For years she taught British literature at the university, and, like me, she continues to read. *Middlemarch* currently. This is a positive sign, and she is in all ways still beautiful. Stately, even, though nowadays much more easily confused and disoriented. And so the reminder notes that she leaves herself read like poems, like the tiny, crooked script of pure metaphor, but the following is not one: the top joint of her every finger is crabbed and canted out in a different direction. It is a wonder that she can write at all, this woman who no longer has enough hair to gather in her hand, the shiny auburn heft of it gone fine and white and brittle. Stick around long enough and you'll see what I mean.

I have endured two knee replacements that allow me to mow and rake the lawn without anxiety or undue pain, and, at my best, to forgo the support bar by the downstairs toilet. Minor miracles, of course, compared with the flight my legs used to take above a pommel horse, hips rotating like ball bearings and my toes pointed heavenward. Now I get around. I sort the mail. I check the weekly grocery receipt to be sure that the supermarket scanner has not taken advantage. Plus I do all the cooking, and weigh fifty pounds more than in my college days when I attended the University of Michigan on a gymnastics scholarship. A full ride and trophies and plaques to prove it. To dismount in any approximation of those old ways would incite the fracture of every surviving bone in my body. Yes, I believe and accept that gravity has finally seized from me all sensation of grace and weightlessness.

Even my breathing sits like rock salt in my chest, which is why my cardiologist has scheduled another stress test for next week. "A reality check," he says. "A wake-up call, Mr. Frysinger." As if the scar connecting my clavicle to my navel isn't reminder enough, how it

glows bright purple under the buzz of those fluorescent tubes, telltale
of the emergency triple bypass I underwent on a Christmas Eve not so
long past. I listen carefully and follow his instructions to exercise with
caution, and geezer-like I swim my easy laps at the community pool.
I swallow an aspirin first thing each morning, and carry at all times
a tiny round tin of nitroglycerin pills like a final act of contrition. If
I were suddenly stricken, I believe my final thoughts would be about
how the arc of the hill behind our house rises and disappears in proportion to the various nighttime shades of light and dark.

This, however, is not yet that moment. It is 1963, and I am floating
side by side in the Great Salt Lake with a woman who is slender and
young and not my wife, her legs long and shapely and sunlit. Hazy
golden, her hair the color of fiery cinnamon. We are holding hands,
our hipbones touching. We have detoured here from the barren and
godforsaken salt flats, where yesterday a man avowing a lifelong death
wish set the world land speed record at 407.45 mph.

Light-years removed from my usual beat, and bored by the spectacle and the unrelenting heat, this woman and I caught each other's
eye and spent the night in a town too unremarkable to recall by name.
But hers is Jeannine Van Maanen, journalist. She is thirty-two and the
first of my three infidelities. Divorced, no kids, and she asks me about
my son, who, when I call, is still too young to come to the phone on his
own. Mary-Helen holds the receiver to his ear, and he smiles and kicks
his feet when I speak. That's what she tells me. She says, "Clyde." She
says, "We miss you something awful. How much longer before you
can come home?"

"What's his name?" Jeannine asks. "Your son."

"Eric," I say, which it is not. His name is Tucker, but I have known
this woman for less than seventy-two hours, and my son is a sacred
continent.

She lifts her free hand and lets the water run off her fingertips onto
her throat and stomach and breasts, which are large and dark nippled.
Then she does it to me, and I imagine I am seeing the two of us small,

as if from an aerial view, the camera lens zooming in. The stretch of seconds it takes, the slowdown, the stop-time, that image of us as a couple forever indelible in my mind. I will flash on it—though I don't know this yet—while Mary-Helen hammers brightly colored croquet stakes into the thick green turf our backyard will, by next Fourth of July, become. And intermittently, and without warning, I will key on this other, perpetually young woman, whose splayed legs glint in the sun, and whose eyes reflect the inexact blue distance of the Utah sky. The rental car is cherry red and the rumble strips loud as I swerve onto the highway's shoulder, where I brake hard and we lick the residue of salt from each other's lips and neck. A motorist passing—never mind how fast—double honks. Followed by someone else. We are their momentary fantasy, a stay against the steady drone of traffic, the shimmering blacktop of late afternoon, the treeless space pressing in all around us. We have earlier undressed in their honor. It is exactly what I would have daydreamed, too.

At the airport I promise Jeannine that I will keep in touch. We promise each other, but I have already lied to her about my son, my motives, and lastly, my address. "Badger," I said, instead of Wolverine, and jotted down for her invented numbers on an invented street in an actual town named Baraboo, where my first serious girlfriend led me into a pasture of sun-bleached skulls, the attached, tipped-up steer horns at dusk nearly incandescent. From behind I slid my index fingers through the belt loops of her jeans and pulled her tightly against me, the scent of her, I remember, akin to honeysuckle.

The day after she dumped me I referred to her to my buddies as a first-class, dumb-ass ballbuster of a bitch, notwithstanding that she had driven across three state lines to break the news to me face-to-face. If I could I would take back every ardent, angry, wrong word I have ever uttered about her or about anyone I have ever loved.

There is a grainy black-and-white self-portrait of me sitting cross-legged in the opening of a Mongol tent, the flaps pulled back to let in the moonlight. It is Mary-Helen's all-time favorite photograph of

mine. A young and content Jimmy Cagney, she used to say, lifting
the silver frame off the bureau top for a closer look. I am lucky now if
some mornings she calls me by my rightful and time-honored Chris-
tian name.

But perhaps tonight I resemble the prowler more than the man in
the photograph as I walk a few steps farther away from the house and
stop and peer back. A single living-room lamp casts its low-wattage
halo partway across the arm of the overstuffed easy chair, where our
diabetic cat George is curled, his blindness a sorrow, I believe, only to
me. Neither Mary-Helen nor I ever mention anymore how his eyes at
night shine a brilliant, opaque bluish white when he stands and stares
as if uncertain of what direction to go, or where he wants to be. Like
me he is a creature of deep concentration, and in this way we are mirror images, parallel beings to the phantom prowler. And this drink
I've poured is no doubt a toast to our collective and insatiable loneli-
ness.

Would it surprise—possibly even shock you—to discover that
I am nonetheless an optimist at heart? Or that I was present at the
original sighting of the angel Gabriel minutes before a malarial fever
that should have killed me broke? Consider this: stars exist that our
night has never seen, but here it is again, a Friday night, and there is a
breeze, and that scratchy music of crickets, like everything that rises
and sets, has already begun to quiet.

If you listen closely you can hear the steady, low hum of our state-
of-the-art air conditioning system. Before its installation Mary-Helen
and I would drive to the abandoned quarry a few miles outside the
town limits, a cooler of ice-cold beer in the back seat. Radio cranked
up, and the two of us harmonizing to Perry Como's "Round and
Round," the crook of her bare arm sweaty and burning on the nape of
my neck.

Even in late July the temperature above the bottomless spring-fed
water would plummet by as much as twenty-five degrees between twilight and dawn. We always brought a blanket, and it was there that
Mary-Helen conceived. As few as five or six years ago she could have

told you at precisely what instant, at what angle of rotation the dashboard clock's glowing green second hand might have paused for a tick or two. Now she becomes impatient and rattled by how to set an alarm clock. I schedule all her doctor's appointments, and I line up, in small paper cups each morning on the table, the pills we swallow to ease our lives along.

On cool, early summer mornings the screen door is sometimes so thick with mayflies that she mistakes their translucent, almost invisible wings for snow. She will pull on boots, a coat over her nightgown. I do not attempt to stop or correct her as she makes her worried trek outside toward the garden with an armload of sheets to cover and save however many roses she can, the organdy of some so dark they appear bruised and swollen faced. But the season, mercifully, has not been foreshortened. The stems are still prickly and shiny green, and I am standing on the porch, speaking her name, saying it over and over: "Mary-Helen. Mary-Helen," like some far-off echo she eventually hears, and, hearing, she turns, her body motionless and backlit so her face is all a shadow, her uncombed hair a delicate arc of rising mist. She is standing exactly where the clothesline used to be, and where the sheets used to billow like sails, the boat of a wicker basket afloat directly below on the grass.

It is as if I have asked her to hold the pose for the purpose of capturing this moment before it forever drifts away. But what if she were to stoop instead and pick up a single wooden clothespin and hold it out to me? Anybody care to take a guess as to how I might react? Yes. I would bury my face in my hands and begin to weep like some oddly familiar stranger she is nonetheless sure that she has never before in her life seen.

For starters, the woman lets down her hair. It is damp and tangled. Late evening and there is a thunderstorm, the power out but the flashbulbs of lightning through the window illuminate the room. Not so much a slow-motion strobe effect as a series of stills, each frame exposing a little more of her nakedness. If this were for art's sake, I would not be sitting so close to her on the bed, the covers pulled back, and the un-latched shutters slapping like wings. No matter how often I shoot and reshoot this scene in my mind's eye, every detail remains identical.

This is the second of my three flings, each short-lived—but then again, what doesn't seem so anymore? And to what do we owe our days, to what new urgency or allotment, to whose skewed version of events? After all, everything is verb, the years advancing while we eat and sleep and make love, sometimes half a world and half a millennium away. Barcelona, this time, though any attempt to map or diagram my life leads nowhere that I can either justify or condemn. I exist in that middle space, and haven't a clue to this day whether or not Mary-Helen, prior to her eventual distant and recalcitrant haze, ever suspected a thing. Or, in the end, if she could have mustered need enough to even care. If so she will take that silence to her grave.

The closest she ever came to inquiring was the evening she glanced up at me at the dining room table and said, absent of any distinguish-able tone or context, "Tell me, Clyde, something inconsolable about you that I could never guess. Some murky reach inside you that you have never allowed me to see."

I had just recently arrived home, exhausted and jet-lagged, my eyes still stinging and red rimmed. And no wonder, given how I had been blindsided by homesickness. And just plain sick to death of the grind and the mayhem, and mourning virtually every second that I had been away, craving, of all things, familiar ceilings and walls, a king-size bed instead of an air mattress or army cot. A neighborhood where nobody has ever been fire-hosed or handcuffed or forced face-down onto the ground.

In answer to Mary-Helen's question, I might simply have overrid-den her curiosity with a shrug. Feigned disinterest, as in not a single dark-cellar haunt or secret to confess or confide, and nonchalantly re-turned to my crossword. Tucker was sound asleep upstairs, and the Greater Dog had already ambled through his nightly rounds to settle at the eastern edge of the Milky Way. We were a family and all together again, and safe from whatever unforeseen wrongs or uprisings lurked out there. No backstory needed, and certainly no conscious will to impose or liberate. No sudden urge to piece together for her a single thing.

So why did I say, "Put down your book"? And when she did, I quietly unleashed in lurid detail how, while flat on my back—an Angolan soldier's camouflaged combat boot pressing down heavily on my chest—I offered up not my passport or press credentials but rather a single wallet-sized snapshot. "My wife," I said to him. "And my young son."

He smiled and nodded. "Do not make of her a widow," he said. "Do not father-orphan your child. Go home." And after ripping the film from my camera, he hauled back and slammed it full force into the ground, inches from my head. "Go now," he said. "The jails here, they afford—how do I say—few American luxuries. Leave while you still can, or you will remain here far longer than you wish."

There was a small group of nuns being detained at the same checkpoint. One of them walked over and bent down and blessed me and kissed my hand, and on the interminable flight home I dreamed of her being dragged away and tortured for refusing to admit to trumped-up political crimes.

These are conditions common to my vocation, but way more than Mary-Helen needed to hear in order to forgive me for whoever I was, what*ever* I might have done, there or elsewhere. The high-stake risks I had run for half a lifetime, and without any serious consideration of ever giving that life up.

"*Which* hand did she kiss?" Mary-Helen asked, and I said, "The left one." And she said, "No, show me." And when I reached into that empty space between us, our fingers interlocked, our grips tightening. Above the table, a garish, low-hanging light fixture that we hadn't yet replaced. I could feel its radiant heat and I noticed for the first time the stencil of lines so fine in Mary-Helen's face that they vanished, as if airbrushed away, the instant she let go and leaned back slowly in her chair.

"Okay. Your turn to tell me something," I said, and without a second's pause she said, "The prowler. He was here again. Earlier, while
you were napping."

But it was winter, an inch or two of fresh snow on the ground, and
when I went outside to investigate, there were, of course, no footprints
other than mine. And behind the glass slider, not ten yards away,
Mary-Helen stood hugging herself, though I was the one in shirt-
sleeves and house slippers, frigid and shivering. A sudden, nervous,
full-body tremor that I imagined coursing through the prowler whenever *he* spied her, in whatever weather, irrespective of season. This
woman with the top two buttons of her nightgown undone, standing
there stock-still, like a sleepwalker or a prisoner in the semi-dark soli-
tude of her own house. Eyes wide open and the room dimly lit behind
her.

I have outlived my two brothers, one older, one younger. My mother,
naturally. And my father, who worked hard and long during certain
evenings after hours as a machinist, multiplying his paycheck times
two or three and bottom-lining for us in a scribble of bold red numerals what he needed—"Good Christ Almighty"—in order to raise three
kids. "Impossible in this day and age. All these mouths to feed," he
would say, that same identical script played out for a week straight.
At which point, lips compressed, he would push back his chair and
eyeball each one of us before storming out again. Nobody dared leave
the table until we heard the heavy door of the station wagon slam shut.
Followed by that brief screech of tires and the rear bumper banging
hard onto the street at the tail end of our driveway.

Most often he would stay gone for only a day or two before cir-
cumnavigating his way back, from where or with whom I never knew.
Whenever I asked, my mother would only slow-shake her head and
shy away, as if unable to formulate even one hopeful, encouraging
response to our current sad state of affairs. To our "reduced circumstances," as I once overheard her tell my older brother, before she

tucked, one by one, her three children into bed. "Go to sleep," she would say to me. "Go to sleep, Clyde, tomorrow's another day." Instead I would force myself to stay awake for as long as I could, whispering aloud, as if in my dad's ear, how the entire household lived in dread of his next outburst and disappearance. How we believed that one of these times he would vanish forever from our lives, never to be heard from again.

And so I understood the accuracy behind the words when Mary-Helen said, "You know full well that you can't be away like this and be a devoted father, too," and opening the bedside bureau drawer, she handed me a condom. "It's up to you. It's not as if you haven't been offered other jobs. Safe, high-paying jobs right here in town. A scaled-down version of what you already do, and where you'd be home with us every single night. You know how much I want another child, but not this way. Not living half my life as a widow or a single parent. No marriage over the long term can possibly endure this. Or don't those commitments apply anymore? When, for God's sake, Clyde, is enough enough?"

In the complex mathematics of departures and arrivals, I concur that Mary-Helen and I existed apart and alone for much of our lives. It is true, even here on this late Indian summer night. Where, in the year 2009, I am standing directly below her window, the vast and endless sprawl of constellations casting loose such brilliance that for a split second I imagine the automatic sprinklers soaking the lawn with starlight.

Is this why my throat keeps burning, my eyes squeezed shut even though someone nearby is crying for help? And someone else is playing a tambourine on the narrow side street behind the hotel where this dark-haired woman and I have shared the cost of a room until just before daybreak. This woman, the final and longest lasting of my affairs, and we have made a lover's pact *not* to fall in love, though I have already folded her brightly embroidered blouse and pressed it to my face. And there is a train close enough to make out its ragged clatter of boxcars, its bulk of iron wheels sparking and pealing back across two and half decades. Do not ask if the muffled weeping that I hear is my own. No one else is around, least of all my son, whom I have also outlived. Unless, of course, you consider how memory thrusts up the dead on nights like this when the ground begins to swell and rupture underfoot. Like right now, and I have to sit down quickly in a chair on the patio before I collapse.

I can almost hear Mary-Helen's fitful breathing through the screen. If I were in bed next to her I would reach over, as I always do, and touch her back gently enough to quiet the house around us. But I have never once, in the ongoing wake of Tucker's sudden death, entered his room. He, a spitting image of me in all those early snapshots I took of him, albums worth, which I refuse to open and page through. His father's son who, on nights identical to this when I deferred to the stars his normal bedtime, would sit patiently on my lap. Motionless, and head tilted back, he would inquire about the twins of Gemini, why they always split apart only to reunite. "Depends on your interpretation," I would tell him. "It's all part of the ongoing story," all those celestial loops and knots, the receding, out-streaming ribbons of orange and blue firelight.

With every next conversion of day into night he would say, "Dad, tell me again, okay? Tell me more." Always more, and I would point in the direction of the brightest arcs and meridians. "Avis Ficarius," I would say. "The Fig Bird. And look, over there's the Bird of the Satyrs, the Raven of Rome, the Rump of the Ancient Lion." Visible or not, they always gathered to stare down on us from those millions and millions of light-years away. The Camel's Hump, the Ram's Horn. Lastly, and right before I would lift and carry him inside and upstairs to bed, I would always pause, the night suddenly incomplete, and ask him, "And?"

"Yup," he would say. "For Mom." And following his lead I would reach palms up into the sky with both hands and then make-believe drape—as if fresh from Mary-Helen's garden—a rose wreath around each of their luminous necks.

I have calculated the nearest mini-mart to be four point two miles distant of us, the highway bypass well out of earshot, on the far side of Memorial Gardens cemetery. And although the parochial elementary school that Tucker attended far exceeds my comfortable walking range, I have found myself more than once standing there by the front gate, waiting weekday afternoons for him. Like the ghost of some little kid's great grandfather, white-haired and slightly stooped but without any apparent impairment of either speech or cognition.

Mary-Helen used to say that certain flowers only bloom in the dark, and as contrary as that seemed to me, it is nevertheless an image by which I am able to more easily summon our son back.

His dying, the emergency room doctor insisted, was as easy and natural as sleep. As painless as leaning forward over the steering wheel and watching for the stoplight to turn green, the radio tuned to NPR and his foot still pressed on the brake. "Whoever opened the car door," the doctor assured me, "might likely have tried to nudge him awake. No struggle or pain whatsoever. Think of him in an easier world now, Mr. Frysinger. A better place."

That's one version. One I *want* to believe, and, even doubtful as I am, one I sometimes do as I sit at that same intersection, engine idling and the light blinking yellow and no other cars about. The exact last place where my son was alive. Eliminate a single mutated gene gone berserk and he is a mere matter of seconds from continuing north, at dusk, the enduring emptiness of the sky suspended above rye fields the color of pewter. Those same fields that he always passed, slowing down for yet another look, on his way home from work. "An Ansel Adams in waiting," he would say, as if tempting me to confine my talents to memorializing local landscapes. The Walgreens wedged in there now among the commercial sprawl is where I also find myself, waiting alone for as long as it takes to have our prescriptions refilled—Mary-Helen's and mine.

And where I think, Tucker James Frysinger: high-school history teacher with a master's degree from my alma mater. Single but engaged to a long-term girlfriend whose face I remember downwind of that pile of burning leaves from which she slow-turned in a certain lovely motion. I have never said so, but I have imagined, at that instant and therefore ever since, dancing cheek to cheek with her at their wedding, her white satin gown cascading down from her bare shoulders.

At the very least she is old enough, presuming her longevity, to have grandchildren, but in my mind Tucker is eternally thirty-one. A number that causes each next breath of mine to flutter and go cold in my lungs. I see it on the day calendar and I immediately flip the page. Every year on the anniversary of his death, Mary-Helen sets the clocks ahead. Or behind—she is never sure anymore—but what does it matter finally, she wants to know, an extra hour in one direction or the other?

I have ceased wearing a wristwatch, each invisible moment as timeless as the next shutter click that stops it cold. Stops the winds in Tiananmen Square and the fireballs of Molotov cocktails exploding in the early, unexpected hard frost outside the Budapest parliament. Stops the volleys of rifle fire and the stampede of wild horses across the Siberian steppes seconds before nightfall. Prematurely stops a heart.

Mine beats hard as I climb the stairs and ease open the door to Mary-Helen's new, disused accommodations. She appears tiny under the sheet, and if her low moans speak the dream she is having, then I am merely the beneficiary of an ongoing grief. Which is why I tiptoe around to her side of the bed, believing that my new knees might accept the full weight of my body, as they did when I first proposed to her, a ring squeezed tightly in my palm.

But I know better, of course, and so I lean down instead, and although I have not intended to wake her, her eyes in the blurry moonlight are open. She is staring directly at me, as if the stranger in each of us has simultaneously made that first intimate move toward whatever long and full life together we might have. I remember the first time her lips parted like this and what it felt like when I kissed them. Lips a man like me would have died for, and so I do not resist as she lifts her head a few inches from the pillow. Husband or prowler, I open my mouth just wide enough to feel the warm, wet tip of her tongue. The kiss is long; it is momentary, while just outside the stars continue to die out as they hurtle in their orbits.

And I don't know why, but suddenly I imagine the careful arrangement of bulbs that Mary-Helen plants each fall as tiny planetary bodies. Yes, an image of things long lost bursting back alive again and again into this earthly world.